I0746675

Noises From the Other Side

TABATHA SHIPLEY

eBook 978-1-7376512-7-7
Paperback 978-1-7376512-5-3
Hardcover 978-1-7376512-6-0

Tabatha Shipley Books

Because of the dynamic nature of the Internet, any web addresses or links contained in this book may have changed since publication and may no longer be valid.

For information, email tabatha@tabathashipleybooks.com

Also by Tabatha Shipley

Kingdom of Fraun Series

Breaking Eselda
Redeeming Jordyn
Training Tutor
Empowering Sawchett

Stand Alone Titles

A Spark of Magic
Projection
30 Days Without Wings

PART ONE

chapter 1

My mother is taking me away from everything I have ever known. It's hard not to be mad about that. This whole divorced parents thing raises a lot of questions for me about what love really is and how you're supposed to know when you've found it. Is it possible to be wrong when you think you're in love? Here's the most important question: if divorce is so painful and expensive, yet seems to be so common these days, why do people even get married?

I remember reading a book once with a girl whose parents got divorced. The book wasn't really about that. Honestly, I don't remember what it was about. I just remember the girl lamenting having two of everything, including houses. At the time, I was probably ten, I remember thinking that was a stupid thing to complain about. I even thought it would be so cool to have two of everything.

Now, driving Mom's new car to Mom's new house with the car full of "only the essentials because we can buy everything else" I totally get what she was upset about. Two of everything isn't going to be cooler. It's going to suck. Completely.

Mom turns the little Focus onto a small street. "See, isn't this cute?" She's being overly chipper. I think part of me knows that's because she wants me to love this idea. But how can I love it? The place where I grew up is forevermore going to be known as "the old house". Someone else is going to live there. My friends are going to drive by and say "remember when Annie used to live here?" Actually, it'll get worse than that, because they'll stop driving by. They'll forget who I ever was.

"Annie, isn't this cute?" Mom repeats.

"It's fine." The street looks like a regular street. Really, Avondale seems to be just like Surprise. The landscaping is all low water, desert-style stuff. The main streets have lights every half mile and cars are driving way too fast. The side streets have more stop signs than are actually necessary and are too narrow for two cars to drive side-by-side if anyone is parked on the side of the street. This particular street we're on now looks like all the rest. Nothing is striking about it at all. Except that Mom's slowing down, which means we're here.

She takes a right and pulls off the road into a driveway that is shaped like a U. I didn't know houses in Arizona actually had those. "What the hell?" I whisper. But the radio is off because it helps Mom focus or some garbage and we're alone in the car. So, I'm guessing that sigh she just let out is her way of saying she heard me and I should watch my language.

The house is one-story, like most of the other ones around here, and absurdly long. Our house—the old house—was basically square from the outside. It was my favorite thing about it. This one is a defined rectangle and we're facing the long end. There also appear to be two doors, one on either end of the big U driveway. "Which door is the front door?" I ask, finally looking at Mom instead of at the house.

She puts the car in park, turns off the engine, and opens her door. "They're both front doors, technically." She stands up from the car and stretches like the thirty-minute drive through morning traffic we just took was a cross-country jaunt. I get the distinct impression there is something she is not telling me.

I push open my door and stand up as she's coming around the trunk of the car. "Should we go in and look around before we bring in our stuff?" she asks.

"Mom, is something wrong with this house?"

"Wrong?" She squints at me. "Why would you ask that? No, it's perfectly fine. Come see." She practically jogs across the small landscaping rocks to the front door on the left and uses the key she picked up this morning to open the single lock. I wonder, for a second, how long it will be before she has a second lock put on this door, for safety reasons. The old house had two.

She pushes the door open and disappears into the darkness of the house. There's no point in standing out here, honestly, so I follow her inside. The living room, which is what I assume we walk into, is a big square. It looks like a fairly good size, empty like this. There's a plank-style floor, but judging by the sound my feet are making I'm thinking it's not real wood. Mom points upward. "Nice high ceilings, right?" I follow the point of her finger. Honestly, it's not huge. But I guess it's taller than the old house. I shrug.

She heads toward the back of the house, along the wall of the living room on the right. There's a closet thing that makes a section of the living room look a little more narrow. "This is a coat closet," Mom says. She spins in the area she's standing in. "This is the dining room." There's nothing to separate this dining room from the living room at all. It looks like one continuous room. No little divider, no light over where our table would go, nothing. I blink slowly at her, not sure what exactly I'm supposed to say here.

Mom ignores me and keeps moving through the large doorway in the wall behind her, straight into the kitchen. There's a stainless steel refrigerator up against the wall on the right. There's a stove on the left. On the back wall of the house, there's a double sink under a window looking out onto what appears to be a small patio and a large desert landscaped yard. There's also a door, presumably leading to the same backyard area. I walk around the perimeter of the small kitchen and stop when I'm facing Mom, who is still standing in the kitchen doorway. "Wait a second," I hold up a hand to stop her from spinning away from this question. "We just walked the entire length of this house up the middle. How do you get to the other half of the house?" I flick my hand toward the side of the house we haven't accessed yet. The one near the wall by the refrigerator.

"Well," Mom rubs her hands together and avoids looking at my face. "It's a duplex."

"What the hell is a duplex?"

Mom sighs. "Language, Annie. A duplex is a floor plan that includes two houses in one. The other side of this wall is a mirror image of our unit. The owner rents them separately."

I resist the urge to run my hand down my face. Instead, I just sort of freeze, the only movement of my face is my eyes blinking. "Annie, it's not bad at all. It's still a house of our own with parking, a yard, a patio, a washer and dryer in the unit, and two bedrooms. It'll be great." She turns around and starts to walk away, "Come see the bedrooms. They're pretty good sizes."

I earmark a few of my important questions for the time when they can be most valuable for my cause. Like asking about the noise of the neighbor when we actually hear a neighbor or complaining about the yard being used by the neighbor's cat once I see a small animal run.

I follow Mom back through the living room to the other side of our section of the house. She shows me the washer and dryer, the bathroom where I have to resist complaining it is obviously smaller than the old one, and the two identical bedrooms where we will be sleeping more like sisters than mother and daughter. Seriously, the bedrooms have one of those entrances where you go through a doorway and turn left for my room and right for her room. They're the same size and even have carbon-copy closets back to back.

This is where I stop and look at her quizzically. "Are you seriously happy with this arrangement?" I ask. Because I can get behind all of this if Mom does less crying here.

She drapes her arm over my shoulder and rests her head on mine. "This will be great. You'll see."

I sigh. "Alright, I'll try to love it," I tell her. I mean it, I really will give this my best shot. Because, what are my other options?

Mom stands up straight and heads to my bedroom window, which happens to look out on the front of the house and the weird U-shaped driveway. She squeals and claps her hands together. "The moving truck is here," she calls. "Our furniture has arrived."

chapter 2

The phone in my hand makes a small whoosh noise. I don't lift it, because I swear my arms are going to fall off if I have to lift one more thing today. Instead, I look down where it sits beside me on the hastily made mattress.

The noise is a text message alert from my absolute best friend in the world, Ciara. Ciara is basically the coolest person I've ever met. We were friends in middle school. We went to the same high school for freshman year. But then Ciara transferred to an online high school specifically so she could free up time to work at the coffee shop near my old house. Ciara is an artist. That's her real dream, to have her paintings hanging somewhere for people to enjoy. The online high school allowed her the flexibility to paint and work. The coffee shop allows her to hang some of her artwork on the wall for sale. So really, it's a win-win for Ciara, who graduated this summer even though I have an entire year left.

I've been texting with Ciara for over an hour and my cell phone battery is dangerously low as a result. I laugh at the gif she sent me. Then I tap to open my gifs and choose the first one that looks sort of like me when I laugh. I think it's the Mom from some show that is like a cult classic now, she's laughing and throwing her head back. I don't have hair that short, but I totally throw my head back when I laugh.

The phone whooshes again. It's this softer noise because the text stream is still open. It's nice, quiet. This time it's all text. I groan as I reach to pick up the phone. Seriously, even my shoulders hurt. We spent the entire afternoon emptying the moving truck and putting furniture in the right spots. I haven't even unpacked anything. I opened the box that had my sheets and threw the bottom one on the mattress, which is currently on the floor because I haven't bothered to reassemble the bed frame yet. My muscles are screaming at me for all the work I've done. I'm actively trying not to think about how much work still needs to be done tomorrow. I blink a few times and focus on the text from Ciara.

So how weird is the new place, scale of 1 to Wreck it Ralph lives there

I laugh out loud at her made-up scale and type a quick response. *It's a duplex in AZ so like a 9?*

But you have your own room. Can't be all bad.

Ciara and I are both only children. We have both always had our own rooms. Besides, who would I be sharing with, Mom? That's just wrong. *But you're not right down the street.* I type.

I know. I'm getting my car soon though. Then all bets are off.

The car is one of Ciara's four big goals. Art hanging somewhere real (she reminds me all the time that the coffee shop doesn't count), a car of her own, a hot girlfriend, and a million dollars in the bank. She's been saving for that car and keeps promising me she's close. *Soon. I can wait for soon.* I respond.

The phone goes silent for a few seconds. Long enough that my eyes drift closed. I don't think I fall asleep. Eventually, the phone chimes again in my hand. I startle my eyes open and squint at the screen.

Seriously, I gotta get zzzz girl. I work at o-dark-thirty tomorrow am. Night.

I read Ciara's text and respond with a thumbs-up emoji. She's already tried to tell me she needs to go to sleep three times now. I'm guessing this one is the real deal, she started with "seriously". She's probably losing patience with me.

I click the phone screen dark and put the phone face down beside me. The house is quiet and somehow darker than the old one. It's weird. The sounds of this house just being itself are completely different from the sounds of the old house, probably because we have next to nothing plugged in to make that obnoxious humming noise electronics make. The fridge is plugged in, although there's not much in it. The living room TV is probably plugged in, I know Mom was working on getting that hooked up. But that's about it.

I take a deep breath and close my eyes on the exhale, letting my head fall back on the pillow. I can sleep here, I tell myself. It's the same mattress, the same sheets, the same pillow. I can sleep here. I take another deep breath, making myself count to four as I breathe in and another four as I breathe out.

A rattling noise starts, which forces my eyes back open. I squint in the darkness toward where my door would be. It has gone back to being silent, but that noise was somewhere on the other side of the house.

The next noise is a muted sort of bang. Maybe a cabinet? It could be from the kitchen. It definitely came from that direction.

Thank God, I think. Mom is awake. I push myself out of bed. All my relaxation efforts were earning me exactly zero tired points. I like Mom's plan. Have a late-night snack, apologize for my grumpy attitude earlier, and talk. It'll be like Gilmore Girls, but at midnight. I love this plan.

Five steps away from my bedroom I'm liking the plan less. I wish I had grabbed my cell phone because I don't know this house well enough to walk around in the darkness. I stand in the doorway to the living room and let my eyes adjust to the dim light coming in the dual front windows. There's a decent amount of light because we didn't unpack any curtains yet and there's a streetlight at the base of the driveway opening on our side of the duplex. It doesn't take long for my eyes to start registering the outlines of the couch, coffee table, and boxes lining the living room.

I pick my way around all the obstacles, following the banging and shuffling noises coming from the kitchen. I can see the doorway to the kitchen when I come around the couch but the lights in there are all turned off. I cross the threshold and flip the switch. The light in the ceiling sort of flutters on slowly like a roommate who doesn't want to be woken up.

The kitchen is empty. Mom is definitely not in here. I cross the kitchen, taking note of the sound my bare feet make on the tile. I file that under useful information to use next time I think Mom may be awake. It was not the noise I just heard.

I step in front of the empty wall beside the fridge, facing

the other half of the duplex. The noise is coming from that side of the wall. I step closer, listening intently. It's a sort of scraping or bumping. It sounds close like it's just on the other side of this wall.

Mom said these two units were mirror images of each other. That means this isn't Mom up for a midnight snack, it's the neighbors. Frustration warms my cheeks. Two years ago if I wandered out of my bedroom at midnight my parents would've either been sitting side-by-side on the couch drinking wine and watching some movie or they would've been sleeping sweetly in their shared bed. Now, I'm listening through a wall to strangers eat the midnight snack that I was on the hunt for.

I wonder, for a second, if the neighbors are always awake this late. Will my future now permanently include listening to my neighbors raiding their kitchen after bedtime?

I decide to help myself to a little treat, making as much noise as I possibly can in the process. Mostly I'm hoping to wake up Mom, maybe have that little chat after all. I use my fingers to rip open the tape of the nearest box, the one labeled "Pantry" in Mom's careful script. The sound of the boxes, bags, and cans being jostled echoes through the extra empty space in the house.

That's when I realize I've succeeded in alerting the neighbors to my presence. The noises coming from next door drop off, replaced by a heavy silence. I pause my search for a heartbeat, imagining a young married couple holding their breath and listening for me to make more noises on my side of the wall. I imagine them holding in laughter, wondering who moved in next door.

Then my eyes land on the box of cheese crackers in front of me and I forget everything else. I snag the box, ripping it open even as I stand up. I tuck it under my arm, careful to hold it at an angle that avoids spilling. I pause at the doorway, throwing a glance back at the wall that is still silent and waiting.

Feeling suddenly very alone, I shove a handful of crackers into my mouth, flip off the light, and march carefully back to my room.

As far as I can tell, Mom sleeps through the entire snack heist.

Chapter 3

Curtains would've been an excellent idea because the summer sun in this part of Arizona is up at five o'clock in the morning and it really wants me to be awake with it. I successfully bury my head under my pillow and score myself a little more precious sleep.

I hear Mom up and moving around at some point. I try squinting at my phone screen but only make out a six in front of the colon and decide that's also too early to be out of bed. I roll back over and squeeze my eyes shut. It must work because the next thing I know, Mom is in my doorway smiling at me over a cup of something. She holds it out toward me. "I bought that creamer you like. I figured you'd want to power through today's unpacking with the help of a dark roast." The scent of coffee beans fills the room.

"What time is it?" I mumble, sitting up and reaching for the mug.

Mom lets me take a slow sip before she sits down beside me on the bed and answers. "Just after eight. I wasn't sure how long you planned to sleep in."

I roll my eyes at her. "It's Sunday," I tell her. Mom has this thing about sleeping in. She's not a fan of it. She believes that we should be allowed one or two days to sleep until we wake up naturally, but it shouldn't be a daily thing. Not even in summer. Usually, she makes me tell her which days I plan to sleep in, so she'll leave me alone. Today is Sunday, which I already know is Mom's day to sleep in, although that just means she may have slept past 5:30 in the morning. "Isn't Sunday one of my days?" I ask, taking another sip.

"It can be if you want." She shrugs. "We hadn't talked about it. How about since I woke you up today, I'll let you have tomorrow." She bumps me lightly with her shoulder. "Besides, aren't you anxious to get everything out of your boxes?" She lazily floats her hand out as if gesturing to the many boxes I have stacked in here, only one of which is open.

I groan. "I need to shower and eat first, then we can start." I throw the blanket I tossed over myself back and spin so my legs are reaching for the floor.

"I'll be in the living room," Mom says. She gets up and heads for the bedroom door. Then, as if she just remembered something, she turns back. She leans a little on the doorframe, trying to look casual. "By the way, next time you get up for a late-night snack will you please make sure you push the fridge shut and turn off the kitchen light?"

I freeze, my hands halfway to a box marked *Annie closet*. "What?"

"The kitchen light was on and the fridge was open this morning when I woke up." She frowns. "Not completely open, just ajar just a little. I'm sure you tried to shut it, maybe it's a bit of a touchy door. We'll both have to be more aware of it, I think."

I turn around so I'm facing her full-on. "I didn't —" I trail off because the box of cheese crackers is still right there, open and next to my bed. My eyes land on it and then snap back to her face so I'm watching as she registers the snack too. "I mean, those wouldn't have been in the fridge. I didn't even open it." I say it before I mentally retrace my steps and reach the same conclusion. I really didn't. I didn't even think to open the fridge.

Mom waves her hand and shrugs. "It's fine, honestly. The stuff was still cold so it must not have been open that long. I just wanted to make you aware, that's all."

The light. The light is more confusing. I remember walking across the living room in the dark on the way to the kitchen. I think I remember having to do the same on the way back, but I'm not sure. My shoulders slump a little. "I may have left the kitchen light on though."

I almost feel guilty until I notice Mom is smiling at me. She doesn't look angry at all. In fact, why is she even mentioning it? "What's the big deal if everything was still cold?" I ask.

Mom lifts one shoulder in a little half-shrug. "We're still learning how touchy all these appliances are. If the fridge likes to pop itself back open or be tricky, it's important we both know that." She smiles at me, that disarming casual smile she often uses to end arguments. "I'm not mad, honestly."

Then I remember the noises, the entire reason I got out of bed in the first place. "I thought you were awake," I tell her. "I got up because I thought you were already having a snack. But it was the neighbors. They were, like, banging around in the kitchen or something."

"Maybe they're night owls," Mom offers. "Was it really loud? It didn't wake me up at all."

Of the two of us, she is the lighter sleeper. Of course, I wasn't asleep when the noise started. I shrug. "I'm not sure. It's so quiet here at night, that makes it hard to judge their volume."

She pushes off the door frame. "Well, we'll both be more aware of the fridge and make sure it's shut. Plus, in the future, if it turns out the neighbors are being too loud we'll just pop over there and respectfully ask them to keep it down."

"I honestly didn't even touch the fridge," I say, quietly.

"I believe you. Which just means one of us must have left it open before we went to bed. Strange that everything was still cold." Mom shrugs. "I guess we just got lucky." She turns around and heads back out of my room. "Go shower and then we'll work on assembling that bookshelf in the living room."

She's already gone and I'm already digging in the box for clean clothes before I realize something still doesn't make sense. If one of us left the door to the refrigerator open before bed, why didn't I notice the light from the inside of the fridge when I entered the kitchen at midnight? I distinctly remember turning the corner and entering a dark kitchen with no sources of light.

I shake my head and decide to stop thinking about it. Because to point that out to Mom right now would only send her back to the assumption that I left it open. Plus, there's clearly no reason to escalate this argument she seems to be happy letting go of. I'll just assume either Mom was mistaken this morning or I was mistaken last night.

Either way, I need to stop making problems where there aren't any.

Chapter 4

I notice the smell of cinnamon filling the house as soon as I open the bathroom door after my shower. I close my eyes and fill my nose with the sweet scent. Mom's cinnamon raisin bread is probably my favorite thing in the world to eat. The thing is, I have to reach really far back in my memory banks to remember the last time she made it. Knowing Mom, finding the bread machine triggered a strong desire to use it. She wouldn't be one for dragging a bread machine to a new house without taking the time to prove it was worth the effort. Whatever the reason, Mom has definitely made it worth my while to get dressed and go find out what's happening in that kitchen.

I hurry to do exactly that, throwing on the first pair of shorts and the first shirt I find in the box. I run my fingers through my hair, hoping that dislodges enough tangles for now because I actually don't know where my hairbrush is.

When I come around the corner into the living room, Mom is moving a box across the front of the room. "Do you think the bookshelf should be over here?" she sets the box down and points back across the front window to the other corner of the living room, "or over there. I can't decide." The two places she's deciding between are along the front wall on either side of the large window.

I look from one to the other and then shrug. "What if we put it over there?" I ask, gesturing to the wall that butts up to my bedroom. "Then we can put the TV on that wall," I gesture to the shared wall between the two units.

Mom squints like she's trying to picture the scene I'm creating. Currently, she's set the television on the wall I seem to want to use for the bookshelf. I walk across the room until I'm closer to the center, near the front door. "The couch could go here, which would leave plenty of space behind it for the bookshelf, walking, and even sitting to read. Maybe we can get a cute reading chair or something for that corner."

She's nodding now. "Actually that might work. We might even have room for a dining room table in this little nook," she points to the weird area technically outside the kitchen but in a sort of alcove off the living room. "I bet we could put a little chandelier or something there over the table, just like the old house."

The little bubble of happiness we'd created, the one where we could both envision this looking like a home, pops. Because she mentioned the old house. An awkward silence fills the room. I can feel myself letting sadness creep in like a thief.

Mom coughs a little. "I made cinnamon bread," she tells me. "It should be ready in about an hour."

I put on a forced smile and nod. "Yeah, it smells really good." My stomach rumbles at the thought of waiting an hour. "Maybe I'll have something small to hold me over."

"We have PopTarts," she offers. She picks up the box at

her feet again, moving it now toward the spot I'd selected. I notice it's labeled *books*. If I remember correctly, we have about eight identical boxes like that. I'm sure it's heavy.

"Where are the rest of those?" I ask, thinking that I probably shouldn't let my 42-year-old mother move them all around the living room by herself.

She gestures to the little laundry room between the bathroom and the living room doors. "I think they're the ones we piled on top of the washer and dryer."

On top of the units, I find seven boxes and one empty spot where the box Mom is moving around must have been. I also spot the planks that will eventually turn into the bookshelf. Mom has carefully set them between the dryer and the wall. I decide the smart idea would be to drag those in and assemble this shelf before moving all the books. I pull them all out, careful not to dislodge the taped baggie full of screws from the longest board. I set them all down in the living room one by one and then stand up, looking around for the bright red toolbox with the screwdriver we used to disassemble the unit. I don't want to have to ask her where everything is, like some small dependent child.

I see a little corner of red poking out from near a box behind the couch. I have to move a few things, but it turns out to be the toolbox. Mom is now moving the TV stand to the correct location. I assume she plans to set everything up over there. "I'm going to put the bookshelf together," I tell her.

"Perfect, I'm going to try and get this all plugged in. The cable company said we should be all set when I called them last night."

I'm not sure if that requires a response, so I just decide to get to work. The basic framework is pretty simple. I screw the two sides and the center support into the base from the underside while it's all laying on what will be the back of the bookshelf. Then I crawl around to the top and screw that on. I push the unit up the way it should be and find the hammer to attach the stupid back, which is basically cardboard, with the small nails. I push that up against the wall and use the hammer to knock the little round pegs into the holes so the shelves can be supported. Mom was smart when we took this apart, she marked the correct holes with a little black dot from her Sharpie. That means I don't have to do the whole trial-and-error process with the line of identically drilled marks to find the right height for the shelves. Thirty-two little pegs later, I'm ready to drop the eight shelves into the unit and be done.

There's a beeping noise from somewhere behind me. I turn my head. Mom is silencing her phone. "Bread should be done," she says.

"It's been an hour?" In all the movement and work I actually forgot I was even hungry. Of course, thinking about the food has me remembering that again. My stomach rumbles. "Do we have to let it cool?"

"Isn't it better when it's hot?" she laughs. "I'll go slice it, you put those shelves in."

I do just that, as quickly as I can, and practically run to the kitchen. She has two slices already dropped onto little plates and they're both glistening with melted butter. My mouth practically waters just on sight. I snatch up the first plate and take a giant bite. "We haven't had this for so long," I mumble around the mouthful. "It's like heaven."

Mom swallows her bite before answering me. "Your Dad didn't really like it."

I drop the bread onto the plate. "What? Really? He never said anything to me. He always ate it."

Mom's eyes stay locked on her plate. "Sometimes in a marriage, you compromise certain things. You and I liked the bread so he ate it when necessary."

She suddenly sounds so sad. I thought the goal here was a fresh start, a new beginning. I take another bite so the sudden burst of happiness out of me doesn't need to be forced. "Well, it's his loss because this is better than I remembered." I shove the half slice into my mouth all at once and chew slowly.

Mom finally looks up from her plate and smiles. "I used more cinnamon." She takes another bite and then reaches for the knife again. "One slice is definitely not going to be enough."

I let her cut us both a second slice and then I use the butter knife to smear them with the spreadable butter she left out on the counter. Part of me really wants to let this go and just enjoy the morning. Part of me has a lot of questions about what really happened between my parents. One day I thought they were fine and the next day they were sitting me down to tell me they were getting divorced. It wasn't like the movies, they didn't fight every day. They seemed happy. How much of that was fake? What signs did I miss? "Was compromising the problem?" I whisper. "Like, did it get to be too much for him?"

Mom chews on her lip a little. I assume she's thinking. Maybe she's cruising through old memories like you flip through a photo album, looking for signs she may have missed too. I see the hint of a smile pass over her lips before she sighs. "Maybe." She shrugs. "I'm not sure either of us remembered who we were as individuals anymore and I think that was a huge problem for your Dad." She rests her hand on my elbow. "He just wasn't happy anymore and that was not fair to him."

"This wasn't fair to you either," I blurt out.

"Divorce is never about fair, honey. You can't tell me this has been easy for you." I shake my head because I would never try to claim that. "Your Dad loves you. When he's back from his business trip next week I think you should go spend a week with him at his new place. Help him set up just like we're doing here. Then you can figure out a schedule that works for all of us."

I like the idea that my parents aren't going to try and hold me to some every other weekend crap like they probably would've done if I was younger. I mean, I'm turning eighteen in three months. I'm practically an adult already. "That's a good idea."

Mom wraps her arm around my shoulder and squeezes. "For now, you can come back to work helping me drag all this heavy stuff around the living room." I groan for effect, despite the fact that I was actually enjoying the manual labor. "Then we can get all the books on that shelf by genre," she adds.

"Alphabetical by author," I say.

"Deal." She laughs. "I can't offer you money but I do pay in cinnamon raisin bread," she sing-songs.

"Sold!" I take a huge bite and she laughs.

"Love you, kid." She kisses the top of my head and

practically dances out of the room.

"I love you too," I holler after her.

chapter 5

"This is my favorite part of this house," Mom says. She tips her head toward the window above the sink she's standing at, the one that overlooks the backyard.

I put the dishes I brought from the table onto the countertop beside her and lean in front of her face. I look out the window from the same angle she is leering. The backyard has a small tree, like a baby palm tree that hasn't grown yet. I wonder if that thing will survive the summer monsoon storms. There's a covered patio in front of this window but the rest of the backyard is just plain rock landscape. Nothing fancy at all. "This sad little backyard?"

Mom bumps me out of her way so she can keep loading the dishwasher. "A window. I always wanted a window over the kitchen sink so I could look out on the world while I was rinsing dishes and stuff."

I give her a weird look. Exactly the kind she should expect if she keeps saying weird stuff like that. "Whatever you say."

Mom hands me a damp rag. "Wipe the table before you go out, please."

I frown. Not because I won't wipe the table, that's the

easy part of dinner clean-up, but because where the heck would I go? "Out?" I ask.

"Yes, you need to go see the neighborhood while it's not a hundred degrees out. You can't go wandering when it's the hottest part of the day. You should go right now. See what's nearby, feel comfortable, learn the neighborhood."

I roll my eyes. It's not a risky move because she can't see me. She's probably looking out that window. "Mom, we moved boxes all day. I'm exhausted."

"It's a walk, Annie. You love to walk."

I appreciate that she didn't say I loved to walk *before*. She didn't mention the old neighborhood. She didn't mention that I walked with Ciara, who lived at the end of the street. She's partially right, I do enjoy walking. It's a simple way to get out on my own without the hassle of borrowing a car and having to find gas money to keep the tank at the level it was at when I borrowed it. Plus, I don't exactly love the idea of sitting here doing nothing and watching TV all night. I sigh. "Yeah, I suppose it wouldn't hurt to see what's around here."

Mom puts the little soap pod into the dishwasher, shuts it, and flips it on. "Good idea. I'm going to read a chapter in one of those books you set up. We can watch something on the TV I hooked up when you get home. I'll even pop some popcorn." She kisses me on the forehead. "If you see anything amazing, take a mental picture so you can tell me all about it."

I already have shoes on. Technically, they're not the best shoes for walking. But I'm not doing anything serious tonight. I'm just checking out the neighborhood. These will work. So, when I'm done wiping the table down, I just head outside. I'm planning on doing a quick lap around, giving my Mom a little alone time, and then flopping down on the couch for some much-needed relaxation time when I get back home.

The temperature hasn't dropped that much. It's still probably 99 degrees, even though the sun has gone down and the wind is lightly blowing. The street this new house is on is not a busy one but there are a lot of cars parked on both sides. I can see traffic rushing by on the busier street at the end of the road so I know the lower traffic here is part of the charm and not just a lack of rush hour.

I make my way up our new street toward the busy one. There's no one else outside right now, which isn't unusual. During the summer months people around here like their air conditioning. We stay indoors unless we have to, like because our mothers kicked us out so they could quietly read their books.

At the busy street, I take a right and walk one street over before turning right again onto a street that looks exactly like our new one. These two streets must have been designed by the same developer at the same time. One difference, it appears this one is lacking the duplex design anywhere. Seriously, I think we have the only one in the entire desert. What was Mom thinking? Duplexes are cute little things that exist on the east coast. That is not something we do around here. Aren't they for college students? I don't even think I have ever seen one in real life before we moved here.

I notice I'm probably about even with that ridiculous window Mom likes so much and slow down a little, making note of what must share our back fence. It's a sprawling ranch-style home, just like the rest of this neighborhood. It's painted in that odd color that is probably called desert sand but would more aptly be named Old Navy khaki shorts.

About three houses up I find people outside. Three teenagers, maybe close to my age, are leaning on an old car parked on the street. I'm careful to watch them as I get closer without looking like I'm watching them so I don't seem creepy. The guy is in black Converse that look a little ratty and what looks like swim trunks. The girls are both in Vans, one in jean shorts and one in skinny jeans. The entire group is wearing comfortable-looking lightweight tee shirts. They're all talking and laughing with no cell phones in sight. Right away I like this old-school vibe they're all giving off. They look like they were lifted out of a different generation, one where I would be more comfortable.

The guy, who is sitting on the trunk of the old car now, gives me a head bob of acknowledgment when I'm one house away. This causes the two girls to look in my direction. "Hi," the shorter one calls. She has a short pixie cut and big hoop earrings. Not really my style, but it works on her face. "You live around here?" she adds.

I point back toward where the house probably is. "Just moved in over there. Like a street over."

"Where from?" the guy asks.

I stop walking right beside the pixie-cut girl. I wait for a breath, curious if they'll move away from me. They don't. "Not far. We used to have a house in Surprise."

"Oh, alright. So you're not new to the heat. That explains you out walking in it," the other girl says. She has her long brown hair back in a ponytail and she's not wearing any jewelry at all. This is more my style since the same descriptors would apply to my chosen style tonight as well. "I'm Cherish," she says.

"Annie." I point to myself and then feel like an idiot for doing that. Obviously, I was talking about myself. I'm grateful no one laughs. "How is the school around here?" I ask. "I mean, once it's in session. Is it alright?" Wow, Annie, may as well go for the slam dunk of stupid. Who wants to think about school during summer break? Plus, I don't want to be thinking about school. It's a sore subject since I have literally one year left and yet my Mom couldn't be convinced to keep me at my old high school for my Senior year.

"It's not bad," the guy says. "I just graduated but these two still have a year. You?"

"I have one year."

"Whoa, and you're going to a new school for it?" Pixie cut asks. "That sucks. I'd hate to change for Senior year."

I frown. "Tell me about it. I was in a photography CTE course that was going to hook me up with an internship this year and now I'm not sure if that's even possible."

Cherish claps and the sound shocks me. I notice, belatedly, that the other two don't react. Perhaps this is normal behavior for her? "We have a photography club. You have to join. Don't you think she has to join, A?"

Pixie cut, who must be A, nods. "Totally. I can't promise an open internship, but we pretty much run the club this year so you're good. The only catch is they make us handle the yearbook because we know photos. But it's not a bad gig."

Laying out a yearbook shouldn't be synonymous with photography, in my opinion. You're putting bad headshots into a grid pattern. It's more organizational than photographic. Of course, since she mentioned it as a catch I'm guessing she agrees with that. Plus, a club sounds perfect. "That would be great," I say. "Thanks."

"Come by next week. We're going hiking. We're bringing our cameras," the tall guy says. "You should come." He points to the house. "This is mine right here. Give A your number, she'll text you a time and all that."

A pulls a phone out of the back pocket of her shorts. I ramble off my ten digits, area code is a big deal around here because we have three different ones in the valley. I pull my phone out when it dings with an incoming text alert. *This is Ali* it reads. I save the number. "Thanks," I say. I notice Ali has dropped her phone back in her pocket like it's not important. I do the same.

The sound of a door slamming pulls all of our attention to the house next door. A guy with dirty blonde hair stomps his way to the sidewalk and pauses to light a cigarette. He takes a drag and then lets his eyes flit around the neighborhood. He bobs his head in our direction.

"You good, Tony?" Guy asks.

"Same shit different day." That's all the information we get from him. He shoves his left hand in his pocket and walks off in the direction of the busy street.

"Your neighbor?" I ask, pointing at the retreating figure.

"Who, Tony? Nah, he's always hanging around here but

I don't know where he lives. He's a mechanic. Got into some trouble and lost his job. Now he fixes cars sort of under the table," Guy explains. "He's a nice guy, but quiet."

There's an awkward silence for a beat during which I consider the best way to leave without being rude. "So, Annie," Cherish says in a cheery voice that seems designed to change the mood. "You like this neighborhood? Like, first impression."

I shrug. "It's alright. I didn't even know they make duplexes anymore. It's so weird."

Laughter, which is exactly what I was going for. I smile. "Right? They're not exactly common," Ali says.

"Worse, it's not even quiet. Like the people on the other side were up banging around at midnight last night making a snack or something."

"Wait, you live in the duplex?" Guy asks.

I widen my eyes. "Yeah." I throw my hand on my chest. "Why? Oh my God are you about to tell me it's haunted?"

More laughter. I'm killing this funny kid thing.

"No, I just thought it was empty. You have neighbors? That sucks. The people who used to own it owned the whole thing," he explains. "Someone bought it and broke it into two units."

"Oh great, so this is a recent trauma. I can't even join a support group?" I quip.

"Maybe you can join a support group for people who heard their neighbors having kitchen sex in the middle of the night and thought it was just a normal midnight snacking noise," Cherish teases.

I cover my eyes. "I do not want to think about that."

This time all the laughter is louder because I join in. It feels good to laugh. I decide if I stick around too long, I'll probably find a way to ruin this. Instead, I should leave while I'm ahead. "I gotta get home," I tell them. "Text me or something."

"Totally," Ali says. "Talk soon."

I take a few steps in the direction I was headed. Then I stop and turn around. "Wait until I'm out of earshot to discuss how cool I am," I holler over my shoulder.

Again, there's a burst of laughter. I smile the rest of the way home.

chapter 6

I finish the block and end up back at the house, approaching from the other side of the duplex. The only car in the big U of a driveway is ours. Exactly as it was when we drove up. Exactly as it has been every second we've lived here, as far as I know. In fact, the entire right-hand side of the house appears dark. The people I just met seemed shocked that I had neighbors. They thought this house was empty. Right this second that half still looks empty. Strange.

When I open the door on our own side of the house, I find Mom sitting on the couch with her favorite blanket over her legs. There is a little chill in here with the air conditioner running and the ceiling fan on high. Not enough for even a thin blanket, but Mom is weird like that. There's a paperback copy of Fahrenheit 451 within arm's reach of her. It looks like she's about a quarter of the way through it, judging by where the spine is struggling as it sits facedown on the coffee table in front of her. I love that book. I hate that Mom put it face down. I look around the room and fish in my pocket, hoping to find something to use as a bookmark. My hand closes around one of those ridiculously tiny nails from the back of the bookshelf. I walk between Mom and the coffee table, snagging the book on my way by. I hold up the nail. "Look, a bookmark that won't break the spine of your favorite daughter's favorite classic."

Mom rolls her eyes but she lets me put the nail in the top of the page, close the book, and return it to the table. I'm sure she'll lose that so I make a mental note to find something more permanent. We used to have a whole bunch of those magnetic bookmarks that clip onto the top of the page. I should find that box before she destroys all my books.

"What are we watching?" I ask because the commercial on TV currently won't tell me.

"Some family drama thing. I don't know." Mom tosses me the remote control. "Pick something."

I let the remote drop onto my leg and turn my body to face Mom. "Tell me again about the people next door. Who are they?"

Mom sighs. Not a little sigh either. This is a whole lungful of air let out in a slow whoosh. It's the sound she makes when she's fully annoyed with me. "Honey, I don't know anything about them. They're renters, like us. I wouldn't want the owner disclosing all my information to them so I have to accept the fact that I don't know anything about them either."

"No, I get that. I'm not asking for their names, or whatever. It's just that I met these kids on my walk who told me the house was empty before we moved in."

Mom turns her head and narrows her eyes at me. "Well, they were mistaken."

"Did you know this all used to be one house? The previous owners broke it up."

"That doesn't make much sense. What did they do with

two kitchens?" She shakes her head. "Is this more information from the local teenagers?" Somehow she makes the last word sound dirty as if teenager is an infectious disease she's hoping not to catch.

I roll my eyes. "Whatever. I don't know. I haven't looked into the history of the house myself. It might not be true. But have you ever met the other renters?" I ask.

"No."

"Have you ever seen them at all? Like on your trips to the house before you signed the paperwork?" I push.

"No." She drags out the word a little, letting her annoyance out. "But didn't you say you heard them last night?"

"Where are they now, though? How come we haven't heard anything else? What if it's, like, a raccoon in there or something?"

A laugh bursts out of Mom. Not a warm, fuzzy one like the laughter from the kids on the next street either. This one is directed at me when I wasn't trying to be funny. This one stings like a slap across the face. "Raccoons in the desert? No." She must notice I don't look amused because she softens a little. "Would you like me to walk over there and knock on the door?"

I think about that. "Yes. That's exactly what I want." It seems like this will all be solved when I see who lives there. Are we talking about a couple of younger people who may have been having inappropriate kitchen sex or are we talking about an old couple who were more likely to have been snacking? I need these answers. I need to be able to put faces with the weird noises next time. Well, unless it was sex noises. I don't need to put faces on that.

"Fine." Mom stands up. "I'm not going over there empty-handed and I'm not going alone. You get a bottle of wine or something from the kitchen. I'm putting my shoes on."

She shuffles off toward her bedroom. I know absolutely nothing about wine so I just grab the first bottle I see in a box and hope it's not like a rare vintage or something. I figure I'm probably safe. Mom buys her wine from a store that always has a deal where you get the second bottle for like a nickel or something. I meet up with her in front of our door, she's slipped her feet into a pair of cheap flip-flops. "We're really doing this?" Mom asks.

"Yes, please." I hand her the wine and follow her out the door. She crosses the expanse between the two doors by taking the paved path on our side down to the U driveway, following the top of the U over, then taking the identical paved path on the other side. She stops in front of the other door and raps her knuckles across the surface with confidence I definitely don't have.

Unsurprisingly, the door to this half of the duplex looks identical to ours. The same white paint that shows no wood grain. The same white trim. I wonder if it's new. If those people I met were right, this used to all be one house and one house would not require two front doors. So which of the doors was the original, I wonder. I can't tell the difference. They look to be about the same age and quality.

Mom taps again, a little louder. I reach out to touch the door frame with my right hand, trying to see if it feels aged or anything. It doesn't feel cracked. It just feels warm, which is the default temperature for anything outside in summer after dark. "Well, I guess they're not home," Mom says. "We'll try again tomorrow." She turns and heads back toward the driveway.

"They haven't been here all day," I point out.

"So they have lives," she calls over her shoulder.

I groan because she is just not getting this. I honestly am starting to think no people are living on this side of the house. So what was that noise I heard?

If I cut across the landscaping rock instead of using the little driveway I will walk right in front of their living room window to get to our front door. So, naturally, that's exactly what I do. Thick black curtains hang down, blocking my view of anything. There's no light leaking through the cracks or bleeding around the edges either. They're just dark black lines of fabric blocking me from any insight.

Mom is impatiently waiting at our open front door, watching me like I've lost my mind. I jog past our own front window and meet up with her. "Satisfied?" she asks.

"No. They didn't answer the door. I still don't know if someone lives there."

"Annie, you don't really think someone puts curtains up on an empty unit, do you?"

I pause for a beat to think about this. I saw the curtains but I didn't think of that. They didn't even really register in my brain. "I don't know. I've never owned a house I was trying to rent."

She sighs. "They don't. As you would know if you use that gorgeous brain." She reaches out and taps me on the nose. "Our unit didn't come furnished or with curtains, did it?"

No. I don't need to say it out loud, she knows she's right.

"So it's not logical to think that the owner only provided curtains on one half. Someone lives there, they're just not home." She wraps her hand around the neck of the wine bottle and lets it hang down by her side. "We'll try again tomorrow with another bottle of wine."

"What's wrong with that one, is it too expensive or something?"

She laughs and inspects the bottle. "No, this one is perfect. That's why I'm going to open it and have a glass."

I settle on the couch beside my Mom and we binge-watch episodes of a show we've seen hundreds of times. It might look like I'm engrossed in what's happening on the screen and enjoying the time with my mother, which I kind of am. But I'm also listening intently for noises on the other side of the wall. Just in case.

chapter 7

Why am I awake?

I have no idea what time it is, I just know my room is deeply dark. I also know that I was asleep a few seconds ago and I'd like to be asleep again. At least I think I'd like to be asleep. Instead, I'm wide awake. Which begs the question, what woke me up?

I lay frozen in bed in exactly the same position I was asleep in moments before, staring at the ceiling. I have no idea what woke me, but my entire body is tense and on high alert. I can feel sweat forming on my forehead. My arms have that cold feeling that comes when all the little hairs stand up at once. I realize I'm holding my breath and then feel stupid. What am I scared of? Who wakes up in the middle of the night for no reason and feels instantly scared? This is ridiculous.

I tell myself to move but nothing happens. I'm still lying here, waiting for something to happen. My brain is filled with that irrational freeze reaction that only seems to kick in when it's dark, that implausible idea that staying as still as a statue would somehow keep me safe from any perceived danger. Seconds or maybe minutes pass and nothing attacks me. Nothing happens at all. There's not a single sound coming from the entire house that can't be attributed to me.

My breathing starts to return to normal. My heartbeat slows down. I move my head a little on the pillow. I'm lulled by the fact that everything sounds normal. I must have just had a bad dream. I take a loud, deep breath in through my nose and let it out slowly. I roll to my side and close my eyes again, ready to drift back off into a pleasant sleep and let this entire experience fall into memory.

The first thud sound is loud, but the second is like an explosion through the empty house. My eyes are back open before the third one and by the time the fourth thud rings its way through my room, I'm sitting up and staring in the direction of the door with my blankets clutched tightly in my fists. I have to react, I cannot be paralyzed this time. I was not asleep. That was definitely not a dream. That was a real noise and it didn't sound like it was coming from the house next door. It sounded closer than that.

I grab my phone off the top of a box nearby where I left it last night and flip the flashlight app open with my thumb. The entire room is cast in bright light that leaves me temporarily blinded and makes my eyes squint. I give it a second and then I start padding my way out of my room. "Mom," I call in the entrance we share. "Did you hear that?"

There's nothing from her room. No noise, no movement. I have one foot over her threshold, thinking I should check on her before I remember the wine. Yes, normally, Mom is a light sleeper. But when you get half a bottle of wine in her she sleeps much more deeply. In this case, I'm guessing it would take a lot to wake her up.

I decide to check out the noise, which thankfully seems to have stopped, and only wake her if I need to. It's strange how much more brave I feel now that I'm standing and armed with a flashlight. I tell myself it was probably nothing. After all, I didn't hear a door, I didn't hear footsteps. I'm probably going to find something lame, like a box tipped on its side with its contents spread all over the floor.

Cautiously, I make my way past the washer and dryer. I peek my head into the bathroom and shine the light around. Nothing appears to be out of place. The medicine cabinet is still closed, the shower curtain is still pulled tight, and the bottles we've pulled out of the box of bathroom stuff are still lined up along the counter.

I walk my bare feet back past the washer and dryer, noting that they look the same as well. The boxes of books are gone and the one box of laundry supplies is still full and unpacked up on the little shelf above them.

My flashlight shines into the living room and I see the source of the noise. There are books on the floor in front of the bookshelf. I shake my head, feeling stupid for getting so worked up. I probably didn't do a great job of putting some of them away and they just fell off. I walk faster now, feeling better since I know what happened. There are four books on the floor, which makes sense since I heard four distinct thumps. I reach out to grab the first one and that cold feeling hits my arms again. In the light of the phone, I watch the hairs on my arms stand up.

I straighten and look a little more closely at the books.

A romance by Burton, a middle-grade book by Stine,

short stories by Patterson, and a thriller by Clancy.

I put the books away today by the author's last name. These four books belong to authors whose last names begin with B C S and P, meaning they were nowhere near each other on the shelves. Even if my mother had taken my little walk as an opportunity to shuffle the books by genres like she wanted to do originally, romance, middle grade, short stories, and thrillers would have been separated.

So how did these four books innocently fall off of four different shelves and land face up near each other on the middle of the floor in front of the bookshelf?

I turn in a slow circle, letting the flashlight hit all the edges of the room. I can clearly see that the front door's lock is engaged and the window is closed. Everything looks the same as it did before I went to bed. I hold my breath, listening intently for more noises. I hear nothing until I'm forced to take a breath and give my lungs a break. Even then, the only sound I hear is the sound of my own deep breathing.

Enough, I decide. I'm not letting myself stand here and be scared of a couple of books that slipped off a shelf. I flip open the camera app on my phone and snap a quick picture. I'll just have that to show Mom in the morning, just in case.

Then I put the books back on the shelf. I notice there are perfect holes where they fit alphabetically. Nothing has been moved or disturbed besides these four books.

Once the books are back I practically run to my room and dive under the covers. I feel ridiculous for the sense of security that washes over me with that simple act. There's a rational part of my brain that knows if there was a real danger a set of sheets and a thin blanket would not stop that danger from reaching me. But my inner child feels safer in this bed then anywhere else in the house.

I turn off the flashlight but keep the phone beside me, just in case. Then, inside the little cocoon I've made of my sheets, I let myself fall asleep again.

It's not a deep sleep.

Chapter 8

At some point during my fitful sleep, I kicked off the blanket. It's now lying in a heap on the floor of the bedroom, which means it is not protecting me from the summer sun coming in the window. I try to bury my head under the pillow, but decide against it when I remember the late-night book incident. Instead, I shove my feet into a pair of slippers and make my way to the kitchen, following the scent of coffee.

I pause at the bookshelf just long enough to see that everything looks completely in order there. No books moved, no shelves tipping precariously. Nothing to indicate anything unusual.

Mom is in the kitchen with her phone in her hand and a cup of coffee in front of her. She smiles in my direction. "Coffee on the counter," she says.

"Yeah, I'll get to that." I call up the picture of the books on the floor that I took last night as I cross the kitchen to her. I drop into the chair beside her. "Last night there was some noise, like banging. I went out to investigate it and found this on the floor." I shove the phone toward her.

She looks down at it and then back at me, quickly. "Books?"

"Yes. Books."

She takes a sip of her coffee. I can't help but see that gesture for exactly what it is. I'm being blown off. "Mom," I let my annoyance color my voice. "This is weird. Look at the picture."

She does, but it's a brief flicker of a look. "Books fell off a shelf in the middle of the night." She lets a little laugh out, it sounds fake. "This is what we get for having too many books. That poor shelf was showing its frustration."

"Four books fell off four completely different shelves at precisely the same moment without disturbing anything near them?" I ask, my voice rising with my frustration. "Four books left perfect little holes where they fell, proving they were nowhere near each other, yet landed face-up on the floor together? Mom, that's totally illogical and you know it."

Now she looks down at the picture for a beat longer. Maybe she's noticing the same thing I did, that the author's last names are not the same. They're not even close. "Did you lump them together like this?" she asks. "To get a picture of them all?"

"No, that is exactly what they looked like when I came around the corner."

Mom takes another sip of her coffee but this time I notice her eyes stay on the photo. She sighs. "Annie, I'll concede that this is weird but that's the best I can give you. There's a perfectly logical explanation in there somewhere." I open my mouth to scoff and she stops me with a wave of her hand. "I don't see the explanation right now either. But I'm not going to be irresponsible enough to think that there isn't one."

"Mom —"

"What's the alternative, Annie? What are you suggesting?" she cuts me off. "Are you trying to tell me you think someone broke into the house in the middle of the night, selected four books off four different shelves, and dropped them on the floor? What was the purpose of that?" Now her voice is rising. I shrink away from it a little bit.

"I don't know," I mumble.

"Exactly, because you let your emotions run away with you." She stands up beside me and runs a hand down my hair. Her voice softens with the gentle touch. "It was late and dark, the noise scared you. It would scare anyone. So your mind jumped to conclusions. But in the daylight, even you can see how ridiculous your fears are. Some books fell off the shelf. Relax."

She pads her way out of the room and I make my way to the coffee pot. I am not normally such a high-strung person. So why did that book thing bother me so much? Mom is right, on the surface. There is no way something nefarious happened last night. I didn't hear a door open or close, I didn't hear feet on the floor, I didn't hear breathing. No one was waiting to attack me when I came out to investigate the books falling on my own with only a cellphone to protect me. The only explanation that makes any sense is the simple one: the books fell off the shelf.

I tip the carton of creamer Mom left on the counter into the black liquid of my cup until it's a lighter color. Then I give it a quick stir and take a sip of the coffee, which is still hot. I pour in a little more creamer to try and cool it off while simultaneously sweetening it even more. Then I take another sip. Much better.

What I think is bothering me the most is that the books wouldn't have landed like that if they had just fallen. I pull up the picture again and stare at it. Four titles all face up. Two of them are even overlapping a little so that one of the titles is partially obscured. So Mom's explanation of the books just falling off the shelf makes absolutely no sense. But, I'm willing to admit, neither does the idea that someone put them there. I just can't think of a logical explanation that fits all the strange clues.

A quiet scraping noise stops all thoughts in my brain. I freeze, exactly like last night, and listen intently. The scraping continues. I step away from the counter and stare at the wall connecting the two houses. The scraping, which kind of sounds like a chair sliding along the floor or something sliding along the wall, continues. I put down my coffee cup and grab the bottle of wine, rushing out of the kitchen.

"Mom," I call as I head for the door. "The neighbors are home. Let's go."

She glares at me from her spot on the couch. "Are you serious?" she asks, her book dropping down toward her lap.

"Yes, I just heard them. They are there and they are awake." I hold up the bottle. "Let's go."

Mom sighs and pushes herself up. "Fine, but Annie this is the last time. I'm humoring you but I have officially lost my patience with this crazy version of you. Do you understand me?"

I nod. I understand that I'm frustrating her but I have

to get over there and meet them. Somehow it feels really important. I feel my phone buzz in my pocket just once like an incoming text alert. I make a mental note to come back to that later, ignoring it to focus on the task at hand.

We use the path in case they are ultra-sensitive about the landscape rock staying in the approved locations. This gives me plenty of time to look around. I notice there is still no car in the driveway except for ours. Fine, I tell myself, this just means they don't own a car or one of them is home alone and the other one has the car. I also notice the curtains on the window are still pulled tight against the light. Ok, they like their privacy. Fine.

This time, I decide to be the one who knocks on the door. I knock loudly so there is no mistaking the source of the noise. I count four knocks and then let my hand fall back to my side. I put what I hope is a "hi, neighbor" smile on my face and freeze, waiting for the door to open.

After at least sixty seconds, Mom turns around and starts to walk away. "Where are you going?" I stage-whisper at her. "They are home. I heard them."

"If they are home then they obviously don't want to be disturbed."

I have no choice but to follow her to our side of the duplex, frustrated that they aren't answering. Mom is waiting for me at our front door. She lays her hand on my shoulder and scowls at me. "Are we done with that now?" Somehow it sounds like an order instead of a question.

"Yes," I hiss, keeping my eyes on the ground. I'm going to have to come up with a better idea for spotting the neighbors than knocking on the door. These people are weirdly opposed to neighbors. So I'll let Mom think I'm giving up on the idea, for now. Until I come up with a better plan.

I pull my phone out of my pocket to check the alert from earlier. A phone number I don't recognize with an area code the same as mine is showing. I click on the banner to pull up the text. *Hi, it's Ali from the neighborhood. How's it going?*

I save the number in my phone and hit reply. *All good here. How are you?*

Good. We're getting together tomorrow night at Cherish's place to watch movies. Wanna join?

I smile at my phone. Before the move, I would've had to check my calendar. I would've had to make sure my parents were ok with me making plans, made sure I had a way to get there, and made sure Ciara had nothing going on. Honestly, I wouldn't have even considered going anywhere without Ciara.

But now? Now I'm not sure if I even want to go. Part of me wants to. This is a chance at real friends in a new neighborhood. But it's also going to be weird. I don't know these people. I don't know who will be there. I don't know anything about them.

Yeah maybe. Gimme the address, I'll see if I can get permission. I respond. That's a safe answer, blame the parents. If I decide not to go, Mom is my instant out. If I decide to go, chances are she'll let me.

Same house you saw us at, anytime after like 5 tomorrow. See you then!

I slide the phone back into my pocket, figuring the conversation is over. Then I head to my room to do a little more unpacking. That will give me a chance to start making this house feel like mine. Maybe then I'll know whether Ali and her friends are the kind of people I want in my life. It's the only way I can think of to start making this place into my home.

Page 56

By ten o'clock in the morning, I'm completely bored. Mom headed into the office this morning after the fiasco that was our attempt at rousing the neighbors. Left to my own devices, I unpacked the boxes in my room, started a load of laundry to find out if the washing machine works, washed the few dishes we had, and read three chapters of a book. This isn't how I'm supposed to be spending my summer. I'm supposed to be hanging out with Ciara and eating entirely too much junk food. By now I should have acquired a new-to-me car and I should be driving it around town finding all the cool new titles by volunteering to fulfill holds at the library in our old town.

Wait, the library. This town has to have a library, right?

I love libraries. There is something completely relaxing about a business that provides jobs, air conditioning, books, and events completely for free. I can borrow books and maybe even find an event to meet people. Plus, don't people in movies always find solutions to the things they're worried about at libraries? Like a montage scene will pop up where the person reads a stack of books or looks at those old newspaper things and finds information about, say, their new house and the weird neighbors who don't answer the door even though they're home.

I pull out my phone and run a quick search for the words Avondale and library. Apparently, there are two. The larger one, which appears to be run by the county, is four miles away. No way I'm walking that far. It's supposed to be a hundred and ten degrees outside today. Way too hot for walking. The other library is only half a mile from here, bingo.

I smear some sunscreen on my face and pull my hair into a ponytail. Then I throw on some comfortable kicks, the kind you hike in but would never be caught dead wearing to school. I grab a big bottle and fill it to the top with water. Then I grab my little keychain with the single key to this front door, drop my cell phone in my back pocket, and head out. Having a destination in mind instantly makes me feel better. I only glance at the neighbor's window once to see if anyone is there. I don't even stare, just glance at the same black curtains pulled completely closed over the same window. Ok, sure, I may look back once when I'm a little way down the street to see if anything changes. But I don't linger with my look. I just glance again, note that nothing changed, and go back to walking.

The walk is uneventful. Everything in this part of the valley looks the same no matter which little town you're in. We have the same types of businesses, the same drab browns for building paint, and the same attempt at xeriscaping. The streets are all wide and full of cars taking themselves too seriously and driving too fast. The lights all have walk signs that blink at you, causing you to feel like you have to run when you're only halfway across. But I make it there without incident and only have to pull up the directions on my phone one more time when I can't remember whether to turn right or left at one point.

The library here is adorable. That's my first impression. It looks simple enough at first glance, but it's way impressive. There are big windows all over the place, filling the whole space with this gorgeous natural lighting. The book stacks are well organized and labeled, making everything easy to find. The paint colors and the chair options are bright and vibrant. It's cozy and ambitious, which is exactly my kind of library. Plus, there's this great metal staircase leading from the first floor to the second. The library I used to volunteer at was a single story. I'm in love with the idea of reading on the second floor. It seems more romantic, somehow.

I wander around the library for a while, taking in everything. I find the young adult section. I find the King books, the new Picoult release, and a Sandra Brown book I somehow missed on audiobook. I don't actually pick anything up. I just sort of run my hands along the spines, like a promise that I will be back for them someday.

The second time I see the nonfiction section I go down the aisles. Nonfiction is tricky because it can be so hard to find what you're looking for unless you have the Dewey decimal system memorized. So you can't just, for example, browse religions. You certainly can't just find an entire section of the history and people of Avondale. I try. I walk up and down the rows looking for the word Avondale and find exactly nothing.

I should go ask someone who works here if they have any books on Avondale. I could explain that I'm new here. It makes logical sense that I would be looking for information about the town. But they're probably busy. Maybe they'll think I'm rude. Maybe they'll be rude, that's the worst. I can't just wander up and make them search for some oddly specific book. I don't even know what I'm looking for. How do all those people in movies manage to find huge stacks of books related to their strange subjects?

Frustrated, I wander back to a cute little table at the front window and sit down. I drink from my water bottle and watch the circulation counter. The guy standing behind it doesn't seem rude. He's polite to everyone who is checking out. He has a decent laugh, one that sounds genuine. When there's no one at his desk he's typing on a computer, but he doesn't look like it bothers him when someone steps up. If I just had a really good excuse to walk up and talk to him, something normal that is part of his job, I think I could actually find the courage to do it.

A pair of guys step up to the counter. They're older than me but not as old as my Mom. One is more corporate-approved than the other, I notice. His tee shirt is clean and inoffensive, his jeans fit right, his sneakers are only worn down in that acceptable way, and his hair is short. He pulls a wallet out of his back pocket and slips a library card to the guy at the counter.

It hits me like heat lightning. Library card. That's how I can talk to the desk guy without being rude or frustrating. It's completely logical that I would need to speak to him to find out about getting a library card. No one could argue with that or think I'm rude.

I push my chair in and hop into the line. The guy at the

back, the one who was dressed less corporate and more casual, turns to look at me. I recognize his face. He was the guy walking out of the house in the neighborhood when I was taking my walk last night. Ali and her friends knew him. His name comes to me quickly and, without thinking, I spit it out. "Tony." Then I realize what an idiot I sound like when he blinks wildly at me.

"Do I know you?"

"Oh, God, no. I'm sorry. You walked by when I was talking to a few of the kids who live in my neighborhood. They just told me your name, is all. I'm sorry, this is so embarrassing."

He swipes his hair out of his eyes, perhaps to get a better look at me. "You're a friend of Ali's," he says. It doesn't sound like a question.

I shrug. "Only met her the one time. I'm new to the neighborhood."

He looks me up and down then meets my eyes and smiles. "Cool." His friend has finished checking out his stack of books and seems to be waiting rather impatiently beside him. Tony tips his head in that direction. "See ya around."

Then they're off and the guy at the counter is smiling at me. "Can I help you with something?" he asks.

Right. I pull my brain away from what feels like a weird encounter and step up to the long counter. "What do I need to bring to get a library card?"

"Do you live in Maricopa county?" he asks.

"Yes. We just rented a place in Avondale."

"Great. You just need a photo ID and proof of

address."

"What exactly would qualify as proof of address?" I ask.

He smiles like he hears this question all the time. "Water bill, electric bill, car registration, any of those will work."

"Right. I'll have to get one of those. Is it alright if it's not my name on them? It'll be my Mom's. Also, my ID doesn't have the new address. It has the old one. Is that a problem?"

He leans forward on the counter, putting his elbow down and resting his chin in his palm. "It shouldn't be a problem if your last names are the same, although it would obviously be easier if she was with you. Honestly, we'll work with you as much as we can. We tend to not give minors a hard time about getting a library card."

"Right. Great." I stand there for a second, trying to get up the courage to ask about the research I'd love to do but can't even think of where to start.

"Do you need something else?" he asks.

"Do you have, like, newspapers or something?" I blurt. Then, to hide my embarrassment, I rush to explain. "We're new to town and I'd love to learn more about Avondale history and stuff."

"We sure do. Newspapers may not be your best bet right away though. You'd have to know what date you were looking for before they are any help. But if it's just interesting history you're after, I can work with that. How about this: you get your materials together for a library card and I'll pull some interesting articles. Then you can come back, we'll get you all set up, and you can look through what I find. I'll also put some books aside on Avondale history. Will that work?"

"That would be great. Thank you."

"No problem. What's your name?"

"Annie." I watch as he writes it on a yellow sticky square along with the words Avondale History. "I'll have those all ready for you by the time we open tomorrow. You come in any time, they'll be behind the counter here with your name on them."

"Thank you." I smile at him, determined to get my information soon. I'll have to remember to ask Mom for a water bill or something. I turn around, ready to take my plan home.

"Hey, Annie," the guy calls. I stop and turn my head back toward him. "You can probably also get some decent information by running a google search. You'd be surprised what you can find online these days."

Yes. A search. Why did it take an adult to come up with that solution? I'm a disappointment to my generation.

Chapter 10

The first thing I try once I'm back home resting on our couch in the air conditioning is googling the address of the new house. That shows me a street view picture and a map. A few of the websites show estimated sale prices and explain that the property is not for sale. I don't see a rental listing, which just enforces my idea that the property must already be rented on the other side. There is one website that tells me the property was last sold in 2017. So whoever owns it has had it for a few years, at least. I would assume that's the guy who is renting it out to us now. I go back to the Google homepage because this is just taking me down a rabbit hole of old pictures of the house that all look the same. No crimes, nothing unusual.

This time I type "banging in night" into the search box. As soon as I click enter I realize this could get me entirely inappropriate search results. The thought makes me laugh.

Instead, the top results are about the actual banging of your head. I scroll down a little way and find people who are complaining about hearing banging in the night. The top suggestions appear to be air in water pipes. I wonder if there are water pipes in that wall. Could that be what I'm hearing?

Scrolling down a little further I find an article about

how you may be having health issues if you hear banging at night that no one else seems to hear. I click to open the article, curious if it will sound legit or not. Apparently, it's a common thing, to hear loud banging in your head that no one else can hear. It's a symptom of other things, like ear problems of some kind. I back out of that, returning to the search results.

The next article that catches my eye specifically has adolescents in the title. I click that one open. Nope, that's completely different. Did you know some teenagers physically bang their heads against a wall in the middle of the night, like sleepwalking? That is terrifying. Back out of that one too.

I stare at the results page. I think part of me expected to find something useful in these articles. Something shocking or perfectly logical. The air in the pipes article, that's the kind of thing I was expecting. Worrying about my health and inner ear problems is not what I was bargaining for.

I close the browser down and grab my book. Better to read than fall into this stressful line of thinking. My phone, which was under my paperback, catches my eye.

Ciara is the person I would normally turn to about something like this. She's level-headed enough to tell me if I'm being ridiculous but she takes me seriously and listens to me. I snatch up my phone and shoot off a text to Ciara.

It is totally weird to hear loud noises at night, right? Asking for a friend.

Then I open the paperback to my bookmark and start reading. I read half a page before my phone vibrates across my lap. It's Ciara.

Not if said friend lives in a duplex and has neighbors. Weirdo.

I laugh and hit reply

But what if said neighbors never answer the door, even when they're making noise? Also appear not to have a vehicle in driveway. In other words, no proof that there are actually neighbors. Just noises. Again … for a friend.

The reply is practically instant. I put my paper back down.

You got ghosts?

Ghosts. I didn't think of that. Ok, maybe I did think of that. But I didn't let myself acknowledge that I was thinking about that, which is the same thing. *How would I know?* I ask.

I'm no expert. Watch Ghostbusters. How did they figure it out?

I think they saw them.

Ectoplasm, she responds. *You gotta go look for ecto trails or whatever. I think they're green and glowing.*

My loud laugh echoes off the walls of the living room. Ciara has managed to make this seem entirely ridiculous and that's exactly what I needed. *Am I making too much out of this?* I type.

Girl, honestly, maybe it's just one person who doesn't drive and is afraid to answer the door. Like a shut-in or something. They never leave the house. Watch for delivery, I bet something will be delivered soon. Even shut-ins need food, right?

She's right. *You're the best, you know that?* I type in response.

I do know that. Gotta get back to work serving coffee to the mildly rich. Love you.

Love you back, I answer. Then I drop my phone down on the couch and grab the paperback again. With the most ridiculous, wouldn't-even-admit-it-to-myself theory thrown out, I'm left with logical ideas again. I repeat them in my head: air in the pipes, shut-in neighbor, inner ear problem, or sign I may be crazy.

I can handle those.

Chapter 11

I'm leaning on the counter in the kitchen later that night, watching Mom cook. Dinner is almost ready now, something I know not because I'm any good at cooking but because Mom has started setting empty serving dishes along the counter. She only does that when she's about ready to drop food into them.

I grab two plates and the silverware I need to set the table for dinner and cross the kitchen to plop them down. We'd just finished talking about the local library that I'd found within walking distance. I told her all about how adorable the library was and how I wanted to get a library card. "So, do we have something with this address and your name on it?" I ask.

"There should be something on the coffee table. Here, stir this, I'll go grab it." She leaves the wooden spoon sticking up out of the zucchini and walks out.

I barely have time to cross the kitchen and make one swipe around the pan before she's back with a single sheet of paper in her hand. "This should work," she says.

I return to setting the table. Honestly, with only two of us, it doesn't take long. I throw out a couple of those round pieces of fabric Mom puts serving dishes on and flop into my chair. I glance down at the paper she handed me. Yup, right address. But somehow I doubt Mom pays this much for water. "Do you seriously spend $100 a month for water?"

"No, that's my receipt for paying the deposit. It'll work for you because it's proof I turned on the water at this address."

"Can I fold it?"

She shrugs. "Doesn't matter to me. I'm just going to drop it in a file when you're done." I fold it and stick it in the back pocket of my shorts. "Hey, maybe you should join a group or something at that library. You should see what they have." She starts putting food into dishes. I stand up to meet her halfway and bring them to the table. "It would be nice to be involved again, wouldn't it?" she asks.

It's a good thing I'm not the type of teenager who likes to argue. I had this same idea this morning, so I can see no fault with it. I don't even mind her thinking it was her idea all along. I smile at her. "That's a good idea. I'll get a list of offered groups tomorrow when I go get the card."

"Perfect." She hands me the plate of chicken. "I'm having wine. Do you want water?" I nod. She fills our glasses and joins me at the table. When Mom reaches for the chicken, I take the zucchini. We each serve ourselves a decent serving then we effortlessly swap serving dishes. Plates full, we dig in. "I'm glad we're still having a sit-down dinner even though it's just us," Mom says.

"What are you gonna do about dinner when I'm at Dad's?" I ask.

Her fork pauses halfway to her mouth, but just for a

heartbeat. If I hadn't been watching her I would've missed it. I feel like a jerk for asking, but it seemed like a good question. Honestly, I could take it a step further and ask what she thinks Dad is doing for dinner right now. But even I know that one would be out of line.

"It'll be alright," she says. "I'll eat dinner and read my book at the same time. Think of how many more pages I'll get through." She winks at me. "I may even read more books than you do."

I let her have that ridiculous argument, only rolling my eyes so she knows how impossible that sounds. Then I load my fork up with food and we eat in silence until half of what I served myself is gone. For some reason, I remember my little internet research at that moment. I swallow my mouthful of food, take a swig of water to wash it down, and gesture to the wall separating our house from the other unit. "Do you think there are water pipes in that wall?" I ask.

Mom turns her head to look at the wall and shrugs. "I have no idea. There's electricity because of the refrigerator." She shrugs. "But there's nothing that needs water on that side." She tips her head toward the sink. "Water would be along that wall, I would think. Why?"

"I just did a little search about hearing noises at night and someone said it could be air or something in the water pipes." I decide not to tell her it could also be something requiring me to visit a doctor. I'll save that for sharing if and only if everything else is ruled out and it becomes completely necessary to take a look at this final option.

She takes a bite of food. "Maybe the noise was coming

from the water pipes by the sink and it only sounded like it was coming from this wall."

"Maybe," I say. But in my head, I'm saying no. Nope, that's not what happened. I'm sure the sound came from that wall.

Mom drops her fork and the sound makes me jump. She pushes her chair back and stands up. "This is ridiculous," she says. "You're not going to feel better until you see what's in that unit, are you?"

I don't know what to say. She's caught me off guard.

Apparently, my silence is enough of an answer for her. She flings open the back door and turns right, disappearing from my view. I get out of the chair and dash after her onto a porch we evidently share with out neighbors.

This is a single concrete patio with a wooden overhang that spans the entire length of the house. There are identical doors to the two units side by side, which only a small amount of wall between them. I look around the backyard, which looks enormous because it's half theirs, and wonder how this arrangement was supposed to go. Did the owners expect the two units to share backyard BBQs on the weekends or something?

Mom's banging on the backdoor of the other unit draws my attention. This backdoor looks similarly cheap-looking to ours. The back doors are flimsier and older than the front doors. No one is answering with noises or words as Mom hammers away at the cheap wood with her fist.

She looks over her shoulder at me, just briefly, then she's back at the door. "I think I smell smoke," she yells.

"What? You do?"

She glares at me. Then repeats herself. "I smell smoke. I'm just coming in to check on your welfare." Then she pulls a bobby pin out of her hair and bends down so her face is eye level with the lock.

"What the hell are you doing?" I hiss. I reach out for her shoulder. She shrugs and shakes me off.

"I'm opening this door because I smell smoke," she says. I watch, half impressed and half completely embarrassed, as my mother manages to dig around inside the lock until we hear a little click. She stands up and pockets the pin.

"How did you even …" I stop myself because there's no answer to the question I was about to ask that would be able to put back the picture of the woman I thought my mother was. My mother is the kind of person who knows how to pick a lock. I'm not sure what to think of that revelation.

Mom opens the door and steps inside. I don't even realize I have the option not to follow before my feet are inside the unit. Shock floods my system as I look up and around the mirror image of our layout. There's the long wall that runs the length of the unit and the squarish kitchen with a few basic appliances. Even the flooring in here is the same except for one major difference, this one is covered in a layer of dust.

I let my eyes carry around the dark unit. There's not a stitch of furniture anywhere.

Clearly, no one lives here.

chapter 12

"Satisfied?" Mom asks. Her voice actually echoes through the empty unit.

"This is impossible."

"It's not impossible, Annie. No one lives here. That's why we didn't know about another renter. Can we please go?" She turns around and walks out of the room. At the porch, she glares at me with one hand planted on her hip. I look down at the two sets of footprints we've made in the dust in the empty kitchen. This doesn't make sense.

I follow her out and watch her lock the handle inside the unit before she shuts the door. It's the same way she would lock the back door if it were ours and, for some reason, that sends a chill down my spine. "I heard noises from here," I tell her. "I'm sure I did."

"You're mistaken. I don't know what to tell you. Sounds bounce off walls, they echo. Sweetie, I love you but you're mistaken. I think you were just thrown off by the fact that this is a duplex. You've let your imagination get carried away with you."

I follow her back into our unit and watch as she locks our door, and sits at the table in front of her half-empty dinner plate. She picks up her fork and takes a small bite of chicken as if we'd never been interrupted.

"You know, something online said it could be like a medical thing. I could have something wrong with my ears that makes me think I heard a noise," I offer from my position in the doorway to our unit.

"I'll take you to the doctor if it will make you feel better. Sit, eat." She takes another bite. "We know it's empty now. You don't have to worry about neighbors. Eat." This time when she makes the command, her voice is hard.

I sit down and pick at my plate until Mom's food is gone. Then I scrape what's left of my dinner into the trashcan when she's rinsing her plate and loading it into the dishwasher. I go through the motions after dinner too: take a walk around the neighborhood, read a couple of chapters in something, watch a show with Mom.

Finally, it's an acceptable bedtime for her. She smiles at me. "Bed."

"I'm just gonna stay up for a little longer."

She takes the remote out of my hand and turns off the TV. "You aren't staying up to obsess about this for a minute longer. Go to bed. Everything will be fine. You'll see." When she kisses me on the forehead and disappears down the hall, I feel like I have no other choice. I follow her.

Three hours and fifteen minutes later, I'm still awake. I'm trying to sleep, but it's just not happening. Instead, I'm staring at the ceiling of my bedroom. My eyes have been wide-

wide-open for so long, they're feeling like the dirt in the desert begging for rain. I've been tossing and turning all night, straining my ears to hear something. Because that's the thing I cannot shake. I'm absolutely certain I heard a noise from that apartment unit. I just don't understand how it's possible.

I turn my phone screen on again. It's now just after 1 in the morning. Mom should be well asleep by this point. I swing my legs out of bed and use the phone screen to light the hallway, just in case. The flashlight app would be too bright if she is awake. The phone screen gives me enough light to avoid smashing my toes on things but doesn't give off enough light to wake Mom.

I am not even sure where exactly I'm headed until I'm there. I stop in front of the wall separating the two units. I lay my palm flat on the surface and close my eyes. I'm feeling for vibrations as much as I'm listening. Nothing happens.

I turn around and spy the kitchen table behind me. The one where we just sat to eat our dinner. At this point, I figure if Mom wakes up I'm already in trouble. I may as well make it worth my time. I crawl up onto the surface of the table, crossing my legs underneath me, and stare at the wall.

If I can't sleep, I may as well wait this thing out.

I stare at the wall, practically willing something to happen. My mind starts to wander. I imagine finding a tiny animal living in the empty apartment, telltale tracks of little footprints through the layer of dust. I imagine the wind blowing the back door open, slamming it into the wall.

When my eyes pop open later, I realize at some point in my brain wandering, I've actually fallen asleep. I bring the phone to life. It's now after 2:30 in the morning. I've been sitting here for over an hour and have nothing to show for it. Plus, my foot is asleep.

I stretch my legs out in front of me, jiggling them a little to wake up the sleeping one. That pins and needles feeling starts and I hold my breath while it passes. Then I hop off the table, pause for a heartbeat to listen for noises that still don't come, and head back toward my bedroom. If I'm going to fall asleep anyway I may as well do it in comfort.

Just after I pass the bathroom I hear something. It's not loud, not even in the silent house. But I freeze, not wanting my feet to cause any noise that might overshadow whatever I was hearing.

Standing there in the silent hallway, I wait.

It comes again. A tapping. No rhythm or beat that I can discern, just tapping.

Mom's bedroom door flies open and her face, wide-eyed, comes into view. "What was that?" she whispers.

"You weren't asleep," I accuse. Then I shake my head, not the point. "You heard it too?"

We both fall silent, listening. I close my eyes to heighten my ears. If it's possible to strain yourself listening as hard as possible, I'm going to have that problem.

"It's nothing. We're just —" Mom is cut off by the loudest bang I've heard yet. My eyes fly open, my heart is beating so hard I'm sure she can see it through my shirt. She holds out her hand. "Give me your phone." I hand it over without even thinking. That sound, whatever it was, was loud enough to shake the walls. I have no idea what could have made that noise.

But I do know exactly where it came from. It came from the wall in the kitchen.

Page 77

Mom uses my phone to call the police. I don't think my phone has ever been used to dial that number before. It's the three numbers every child in America knows and prays they never have to use. "My name is Suzanne Lewis. I live in half of a duplex, the other half is empty and unrented. We are hearing noises in that unit. I'm worried someone may have broken in. Can you please send an officer to investigate?" She rambles off the address then she tries to smile at me like that will calm me down. In the dark of the early morning, it's not exactly reassuring.

She hangs up my phone and wraps her arm around my shoulder, pulling me close. "We have to wait but someone should be here shortly. I told her we were fine waiting. Let's go to the living room."

I want to. But my feet don't seem to want to. My feet seem to want to stay planted right here in the hallway far away from that noise.

I turn my head and look back in the direction of the kitchen. "There hasn't been another sound," I say quietly. Still, my voice sounds loud in the quiet house. "It was loud, right?" I ask. "Louder than I'm talking right now."

Mom nods. "Let's go sit on the couch and wait for the officer." She uses the arm draped around me to direct me to the living room and gently pushes me down onto the couch cushion. Then she takes her time carefully arranging her feet underneath her when she sits beside me. "Everything will be fine," she says. "I bet someone just got into that empty unit. The noise we heard was probably someone dropping something or bumping into a wall." She squeezes my shoulders in a comforting way. "But it's quiet over there now. I bet they're gone. I bet they knew they made too much noise and took off running."

"Did you lock that door?" I ask. What if this is our fault? What if we left that back door open and someone just walked right in. But I saw her lock it, didn't I?

"Yes, I locked it."

Lights flash by the front window as the police car pulls into the driveway. Mom gets up off the couch and goes out front. I follow her but I stop in the doorway. I see them whispering to each other. There are two officers, I realize. The second one gets out of the car and makes his way to the front door of the other unit, shining his flashlight around the door. Then he heads down the side of the house, moving toward the backyard.

Curious, I follow. I'm definitely feeling more confident by the arrival of the good guys. At our back window, I see him enter the backyard. He spends some time at the back door, the flashlight beam shining there.

Mom and the other officer come around into the

backyard and that makes me feel like I have permission to open our back door. Immediately sounds of the world make their way inside. "Sign of a forced entry here," one officer says.

The officer beside Mom puts a hand on her shoulder. Not in a comforting way. More of an I'll-push-you-out-of-the-way-if-I-have-to way. "Ma'am, I'm going to need you to step back inside your residence."

She takes a step toward the house but doesn't fully enter. I take a step outside. Now we're beside the officers. From here we can still see the back door of the other unit but we're technically on our property. We watch as they talk into their radios, giving someone back at the precinct the details of what they're about to do. Then the guy closest to the door shoulders it open. The old wood doesn't put up any kind of fight at all.

"Do you think we were the forced entry?" I whisper. I'm worried there was another one that we missed. Maybe someone was in that unit before we were. Maybe someone has been sleeping there for days, making that noise I heard. I'm almost hoping Mom says we were the issue because that would mean we were the only people who have been in there. Instead, she shrugs as if she doesn't know either.

The first officer steps into the doorway and shines his flashlight around. The second officer steps up behind him and they both disappear inside. I notice the footsteps are loud, echoing back out into the night. But they're not as loud as the bang we heard. At least, I don't think so.

When the footsteps have sort of receded away from us, I risk taking a few steps closer. The kitchen looks exactly like we left it. Dark, empty, and covered in a layer of dust. The multiple sets of footprints from us and the officers have all sort of blended together in a line of wear and tear that leaves the floor looking like a mop commercial "before" shot. The cabinets are all still closed, the counters are still dusty. Nothing appears to have changed at all from our previous excursion into the house.

I see flashlight beams dancing across the living room wall and duck back out toward Mom before I can be caught in the doorway. "Anything?" she whispers.

I shake my head. "It looks exactly the same."

When the officers emerge one of them heads directly for us while the other one busies himself at the back door. "There are footprints and disturbances throughout the house, but it appears that no one is there at the moment. Do you have a way to get a hold of the landlord?" he asks.

"Yes, I have his phone number," Mom answers.

"Someone should call him. He'll want a copy of the report my partner is writing up and he'll need to get this back lock changed. I see signs that someone messed with that lock, but I can't tell how recent that damage was."

"I'd rather call him myself. I'll wait until a decent hour of the morning rather than wake him unless you think this is an emergency," Mom says.

The officer smiles. "I think the emergency has passed. As I said, there is no one in the unit and I don't see any damage."

The other officer appears at his shoulder and hands off a slip of paper. "I got the lock engaged again, but it's not great. Keep an eye on this door if you can. Here's the report." His voice is harsh, clipped.

"Thank you," Mom says, closing her hand around the piece of paper. I don't get a good look at it before she drops it to her side but what I do see surprises me. Somehow I didn't expect police reports to look so much like forms. Little boxes everywhere as if what happens can be easily filed no matter how heinous it is.

We follow the officers to the side of the house and watch as they walk to their car. They sit inside but make no moves to leave. "What are they doing?" I ask.

"I think they're finishing up some recording, maybe." She slips her arm around my shoulders. "I don't think we need to stand here and watch them." She guides me to turn around and head back toward the house. She pauses outside the back door of the empty unit. "He did say to keep an eye on this door." Her voice is somehow distant like her mind has wandered off.

I elbow her lightly in the side. "Can we do that from our kitchen? There's coffee in the kitchen," I say.

She doesn't answer, just follows me through our door, her hand on my back as if she is the one guiding me back inside. We leave our back door open as we make the coffee. My ears are strained for any sounds from the other unit or the back porch. I don't know what I'm listening for, but I'm listening. I hear when the police car finally starts up and when it pulls out of the driveway. When the coffee is done Mom closes the back door and drops into a chair that gives her a view of the backyard through the window. I sit in an empty chair beside her. My view is slightly off, but I can see the yard if I lean in a little.

We sit there until the sun comes up, sipping coffee and watching the yard. We watch the sunlight change as the day breaks, which makes me want my camera real bad. Nothing else happens. More importantly, there is no more noise from the other unit.

chapter 14

After the sun is fully up and the coffee pot is empty, Mom reaches for her cell phone, charging nearby. "I need to go call the landlord. Then I need to shower and get dressed if I'm going to work." She frowns at me. "Are you fine staying here?"

"Yeah, I'm fine." The sun is up now, making everything somehow seems safer. I'm almost embarrassed by how scared I was last night. "I'm going to hang out here today so if someone needs to come by and fix that lock they can."

"The landlord will probably need to call a locksmith, I doubt he can rekey that door on his own."

"Whatever. I'm here."

She nods at me and disappears into the other room to make her call. I stand up and stretch, popping my neck. I hear the sound of a car out front and make my way toward the window in time to see a delivery van driving away. I pull open the front door and find a box. "Did you order something?" I mouth to Mom, who is nearby on the phone. She shakes her head.

I pick the box up, frowning at it. The label is for Annie Lewis. There's no return address, just a company. "It's for me," I tell her. She just nods.

I push the door shut with my foot, already heading for the kitchen and a pair of scissors that might cut through this tape. I slice it open and peer inside. Nestled among those big clear balloon things that packing companies are using now is a black 100mm Macro lens. Immediately, I know who this package is from.

Mom appears in the doorway. "So what was in the package?" she asks, setting her phone down on the counter.

"Remember that lens I wanted? The one I used to borrow from the school all the time?" I point to it. "Dad bought it for me."

Mom's eyes go wide and she leans in to look over my shoulder. I still haven't touched it, so it's just sitting there staring back at us. "Those are over six hundred dollars," she whispers.

"I know."

"They're hard to find, too. You can't just walk into a store and buy them."

"I know."

She looks at me again, her eyes are still wide. "You've been wanting one forever."

"I know."

"Wow, that was really nice of him. I wonder where he got the money for that."

I blow an audible breath out of my nose. "I have no idea."

"Well, are you gonna try it out?" She asks, her voice coated with excitement.

I reach into the box and carefully pull out the lens. It's beautiful. It's not any heavier than my other lenses, but it's so much more unique. This is probably the most expensive thing I own right now. My camera, a decent enough Canon, came in a package with two lenses. A standard 18-55mm and a zoom 75-300mm. Both of those lenses are pretty common. There were a few other lenses the school would let you check out from time to time if you were in the photography program. My favorite was the Macro lens, specifically for macro photography which is the process of extreme closeups. It is my absolute favorite type of picture. Now, I'm holding that power in my hands without having to sign a release form for the first time.

Mom kisses me on the forehead. "Well, I guess we know what you're going to be doing all day. The landlord will probably come by at some point this morning but the locksmith won't be here until sometime in the afternoon. The locksmith is supposed to leave a copy of the key for the empty unit's backdoor with us or at our back kitchen door so that we have a spare, per the landlord's orders." She nods. "Now that you're all caught up on the plan, I'm getting in the shower."

I head to my bedroom, find my camera case in my closet, and lovingly pull it out. The case I have is padded and has four compartments for things besides the camera. My lenses are currently occupying two of those spaces. The other ones were sad and empty. I carefully drop the macro lens into one of them and smile at the way the case just looks more complete now. I suppose I'll need to start looking into what lens I want next. What will occupy that fourth spot? Christmas lists will need to be updated, after all.

I slip the lens back out and pull the camera out. They snap together like they were made for each other, which I suppose they were. Then I hold it up to my eye and play around with a few settings. I snap off a few shots just to see what works and what doesn't. Low light is a problem with this lens, but I knew that from using it before. I slip into my kicks and take the camera outside, where I know it will do its best work.

At some point, while I'm lying flat on my back under a tree trying to get a perfect shot of leaves, I hear Mom open the back door and yell something to me. I catch the words "work" and "love". I holler back at her to "have a good day", fairly confident she said she was leaving. I hear the door shut again and put all of my attention back on the leaves.

The lens is amazing. Even from this vantage point, under the tree, I'm getting details in the leaves that I wouldn't have imagined. I just need to wait for the light to be in exactly the right spot for the picture I have in my head. It's close. Another five minutes, maybe, and it'll be exactly what I'm thinking.

I snap the picture three times before I finally get up and stretch my back and arms out. I'll have to look at them later once I'm inside, but I think I got the shot. I walk around the backyard slowly, taking in every tree and bush trying to find something else to frame with the new lens.

It doesn't take me long to find exactly what I was looking for. A small beetle climbing a branch. I crouch down and use the camera to frame the little guy.

I'm interrupted what feels like a short while later by a man who looks like he's the same age as my Dad. This guy is wearing jeans, a polo shirt, a full beard, and a scowl. "Did you hear me?" he says. The tone of voice makes it clear he is not happy.

I stand up, frowning at the missed shot. "Sorry, no. Can I help you?" I take a step back, putting space between me and this stranger.

He sighs. "I'm Alex, the landlord. Are you Ann?"

"Annie," I correct. "Sorry, I was trying to get a picture. I get a little focused." I step closer and offer him my hand. "Thanks for coming out today."

"Yeah, no problem." He shakes my hand for exactly two pumps and then drops it. His head tips toward the empty unit. "That unit has been a pain since I bought it. I'm sorry it gave you trouble. The cops said there was no sign of anyone inside, just the forced entry." He sighs. "Maybe you and your mother scared someone off."

"We heard something from inside the unit though."

"That's what your Mom said. But I guess they left. I'm going to pop in there and have a look around, but I wanted to make sure I told you I was doing that. I didn't want you thinking someone was in there." There's sort of a mischievous glint in his eye that makes me think he's making fun of me. "I'll just let myself in the back door." He holds up a set of keys and turns to walk toward the unit.

I stand where I am, near the back fence, and wait. He's inside the unit for maybe ten minutes and then he's back. I watch him pull the door shut and use his key to re-lock it. He waves in my direction. "Exactly like they said. I should probably get a cleaning crew in there for all that dust. I haven't exactly been in a hurry to get it cleaned up since no one is interested in renting it."

I bite my tongue to keep from telling him people may be more interested in renting it if it was cleaned and ready. What do I know?

"I'm gonna run. Did your mom tell you the locksmith is coming by this afternoon?"

"Yes."

"Great and he should leave you a copy of the key."

"Right, she said that too."

He shuffles his feet for a few seconds like he's nervous. "Thanks for keeping an eye on the door last night," he says. "I'm sorry the unit has been a problem."

"It's fine," I say. I'm not entirely sure it is fine, that unit has been a huge hassle. But, in the scheme of things, he's doing his best and I feel terrible seeing him so nervous. It's not his fault someone tried to break in. Plus, he's doing his part by getting a new lock on the door.

"Right, well, thanks for hanging around to wait for the locksmith too. I have to run. Nice to meet you."

I wave at him but turn back to the bush before he's even out of sight. Unfortunately, my lighting has slipped away now. I'll have to find a new shot.

Before I get back to that, I decide it's a good time for a drink break. I head inside, fill myself a glass of water from the sink, and take a huge sip. I'm staring out the window at the back of the houses that might belong to Ali or that other girl from the neighborhood, Cherish, I think it was. That triggers the memory of being invited to watch movies tonight. Except I'm exhausted. Mom and I barely slept last night. I'm not sure the first impression I want to give kids from my new school is that I fall asleep during movies. I pull out my phone and hit the text message stream from yesterday. *Hey, not gonna be able to make it tonight. Invite me again later?* I send.

I take another sip of my water before the reply comes in. *Yeah, no problem.*

Perfect. I grab my camera, leave the water glass inside, and make my way outside again. I think I've spotted good light falling on a couple of decent rocks. Maybe I'll get lucky.

Chapter 15

When the locksmith finally arrives, I've given up on the heat of the day and have retired to the couch. Ciara and I have been texting off and on for about an hour when I hear a vehicle pull in. I stand up and peek out the window. The van is white, with a large A&J Locks sticker clearly visible on the side. I pocket my phone and go out the front door. The driver steps out of the van, letting me take in his appearance. He's wearing a blue polo shirt with the same logo as the van. He looks clean-cut, sort of a socially acceptable boss kind of figure. Of course, I watch enough scary movies to know that could just be part of his shtick.

He walks around to the back of the van where there are two doors. He throws both open and disappears from my view as he digs around. I stay where I am on my front porch and decide to use my loudest voice when I talk. If any of the other neighbors on this street are inside their houses, I want them to know what's going on. "Hi," I yell. "I'm Annie, you must be the locksmith. I was waiting for you. The lock is on the back door of the empty unit. I'll walk you around to the backyard when you're ready."

He steps back so he's visible and sort of nods in my

direction but he doesn't say a word. Then he reaches inside the open doors, grabs some tools, and kicks the doors shut. That done, he stands like a silent statue waiting for my next move. I cross the front of the empty unit quickly and turn toward the backyard. He follows me around the side of the house. I make sure to walk fast, which puts a decent amount of space between us. When we get to the back, I point to the correct door. He steps up to it, crouching down to be face to knob with the handle. I leave him there and step back toward my half of the porch. My phone vibrates with an incoming text.

It can't be that bad. Give it time. Ciara, responding to my complaints about the new neighborhood.

I roll my eyes. Then, because she can't see that, I send her the eye roll emoji. I follow it up with a text. *It's been four days that feel like an eternity.*

Four days ain't no thang.

I snap a picture of the locksmith outside the door and send it to her. *At least this guy finally showed up.*

Hey so new locks mean nothing else crazy can happen. That's a good thing.

This is followed by the little ellipsis which means Ciara is still composing another thought. I wait.

Plus don't you have a Dad weekend coming up or something? How does that work?

I want so much to call her right now because this is not a conversation I want to fit into text bubbles. But Ciara is at work. She's texting me below the cash register at the coffee shop while her boss is accepting a delivery. She absolutely cannot answer her phone right now and she would be so mad at me for trying unless it was truly an emergency. Explaining the whole divorced situation is not an emergency. So I try to make it fit in a text.

It's not exactly like on TV. He's on a work travel thing right now. He'll be back in two weeks and I'm supposed to go there and help him set up the new place. I haven't actually talked to him so I don't have the details yet.

It takes her a while to respond. I have enough time to watch the process happening next door lead to a big circular hole in the door where the handle used to be. Then my phone vibrates.

You can make it two weeks especially now that you know there's no one next door and no more break-ins.

A banner pops up at the top of my phone. Incoming call from a random number. Ignore. *Yeah, true.*

Oops GG

I don't respond. GG means Ciara just spotted the manager coming back in. Her phone needs to go silent. That means I cannot text back or it would dance across the shelf under the register, ratting her out. She'll wait until it's safe to be seen with it and drop it back into her pocket. But I have to give her a few minutes. She's already been written up for her cell phone usage once and she needs this job.

I click over to my missed calls and check that number again. I definitely don't recognize it. I'm about to flag it as spam but my phone dings with a voicemail.

I clicked on it.

2 minutes and 17 seconds. But the transcription of the message is not available. I frown at the phone screen and click

on the message. Silence.

I click ahead to about 45 seconds into the call and listen again. Still silent. Confused, I drag the call up past the 1 minutes 30-second mark and listen. This time I close my eyes and focus on listening. It's not a silence that has background noise at all. It's like someone called me with the phone muted. I push the progress bar up to the two-minute mark and listen to the final 17 seconds. Then I hit the delete button when I still don't hear anything. Weirdest spam call ever.

"Alright I'm all done here," the locksmith says. It's the first words he's said to me and I'm a little startled by how deep his voice sounds in the empty backyard. He stands up and drops the old handle into his bucket of tools. "I was told to leave the front lock alone. I guess the realtor has that key." He holds out a single key to me, it's not even on a key ring. "I'm supposed to leave this with you."

I drop my phone in my pocket, cross the porch, and accept the key. "Thank you." I decide I'll have to find a key ring that's not in use and put this key somewhere safe.

"No problem. You have a nice day and tell your landlord I'll send him my invoice."

"Sure." I don't bother telling this guy I don't speak to the landlord. He goes out along the side of the house, back the way we came, and I head inside the back door. I cross to the front window so I can watch him leave without being too creepy about it.

Then I take the key into the little room with the washer and dryer where Mom has put a key rack. She had this whole rationale for putting it here. Apparently, because it's at the center of the house away from all doors and windows it was the safest place to store our spare keys. I find an old key chain that happens to have nothing on it. Judging by the faded plastic jumping dolphin, I would guess it was from our one trip to Florida when I was a kid. I put the neighboring unit's key on the key chain and hang it back on the peg.

Then I settle down on the couch with a paperback book, intending to finish out my day with absolutely no weirdness. In reality, I'm asleep within fifteen pages.

chapter 16

It wouldn't be accurate to say Mom woke me up when she got home from work. It's more like the sound of Mom opening the front door woke me up. I rub my eyes, stretch, and try to pretend like I wasn't just napping when my exhausted mother has been at work. I'm pretty sure it fails because she frowns at me. "Sorry, it was a long night. I guess I just zonked out there," I say with a matching frown.

"Did the locksmith come?"

"Yes. I put the key on the little dolphin keychain that was hanging on the rack."

"Did you put it back on the rack?" she asks, her eyes flashing with an annoyance that can only come from being up most of the night and then working all day.

I bite back my sarcastic retort that likely would've had something to do with shoving it somewhere inappropriate. Instead, I offer her a small smile. "Yes."

"Good." She drops her purse onto the table beside the couch. "I'm too tired to cook. Do you want to go somewhere or order something?"

Technically I'm dressed. Of course, I'm wearing a pair of comfortable shorts that were never intended for the outside world to view and a t-shirt that, upon inspection, may be see-through. "Order." I pull my phone out and open up the delivery app that will tell me what is near the new house.

Three arguments about food and one strong mother veto later, we have ordered pho. It should be at the house in thirty minutes. I stand up and stretch. "I'm taking a shower since we have a little time."

Mom puts her feet on the cushion I've vacated. "I'm going to get one of those relaxing little naps in. Wake me when the food gets here." I'm pretty sure she's asleep before I'm out of the room.

The rest of the evening passes in beautiful simplicity. Mom is significantly less cranky after her short nap, the pho is delicious, and a couple of funny sitcoms puts us both in a good mood. We're in bed at a reasonable, if not ridiculous, time and I'm asleep before you can say bumps in the night.

"Rise and shine, sleepy head," Mom says.

It takes me a heartbeat to realize that sound is Mom's real voice and not something in a dream. I blink in confusion at the doorway of my room. "It's morning already?" I ask.

Mom laughs. "Get up and come have some coffee with me. That will wake you up."

I sit up fully. "Seriously, there were no noises or anything last night. This is the first night I think I've slept without disruption since we got here," I tell her.

"Changing those locks worked wonders. Coffee," she repeats.

"You know what, I'll make it." I know my mom likes to start her day with a hot shower and a hot cup of coffee. Judging by the fact that she's still in her pajamas, she hasn't had either of those yet. I really am feeling more refreshed and energetic than I have since we moved in. I made it through the entire night without hearing banging on the walls, books falling off shelves, or strange late-night snacking noises from the empty unit. I feel like I could run a mile right now. I throw the sheets off and stand up. "You jump in the shower and I'll brew the coffee."

Mom smiles. "You don't have to tell me twice," she says. "You got yourself a deal."

On my way to the kitchen, I check my phone and shoot off a text to Ciara. *Guess who actually slept the entire night?* Then I realize that makes me sound like a literal infant and shoot off another text as an explanation. *No weird noises at all!*

I look up from my phone as I flick the kitchen light switch on with my elbow.

The entire counter closest to me is covered in something white.

"What the hell?" I put my phone down on a clean surface and move closer. It's a white powder. Judging by the open bag beside it, it's flour. That on its own is bad enough. It's a huge mess and I definitely don't feel like cleaning it.

But that's not the worst part.

The worst part is that it looks like someone dragged their finger through it. Written in the flour on the counter are what looks like the letters E U followed by the word DANGER.

I leave the flour exactly where it is on the counter, giving it a wide berth as I step around it. I tell myself this is because I need coffee to deal with it but it's really because I want my mother to see this. Enough is enough. Something strange is going on. Those books couldn't have just fallen onto the floor on their own the other night. This definitely didn't write itself. She has to see this.

So, I make coffee. When I hear the shower shut off I fill two mugs and add a splash of creamer to each one. Then I prop myself casually on the counter directly across from the flour mess and try to look nonchalant when my mother saunters in wrapped in her bathrobe. "What kind of creamer did you —" she starts. I notice the second her eyes see the mess. They get wide and then they turn in my direction. I almost laugh at how accusatory they look. As if I would do that. "What is this?" she asks.

"I was going to ask you the same thing. Have some coffee." I gesture at the cup. "This was here when I came out here this morning. Want to try and tell me what you think happened?"

"Annie, did you do this? Is this a joke?"

"Jesus, Mom, on what planet would this be funny?"

"Language," she says almost automatically. "It's not funny. It's a mess. It's …" she trails off, clearly unable to come up with another word.

"Scary?" I offer.

She crosses to me and takes the coffee. Even as she takes her first sip, her eyes stay locked on the mess as if it's about to do something interesting. "It is a little weird," she says. "We store that flour in the cabinet. If it fell out, why isn't the cabinet open?"

"Really?" My voice rises with my frustration. "That's your problem? Not the fact that there are letters written in the flour?" I slam my cup down so I can cross the floor and point to the message. "DANGER," I read. "It clearly says the word DANGER."

Mom winces at my tone. Then she sets the cup down and rubs her face. "Ok, ok." She holds her hands out in front of her. "There's got to be a simple explanation for this."

"Maybe whoever went into the unit next door came here," I offer. "We already know someone was in there. What if they were in here?"

She shakes her head. "No. No. We would've heard something. We would've seen signs."

I point at the flour-covered counter again. As if to say hello, this is your sign calling.

"I mean signs of forced entry," she clarifies. "Who would break in to write a creepy message and then leave?" She pushes herself off the counter and comes toward me. "No. This is ridiculous. Someone is trying to scare us or one of us was sleepwalking or something. Enough. I'm not doing this." She wets the dish rag at the sink and tosses it in my direction. "Can you clean it off while I get dressed?" she asks. "I'm done with whatever this is."

"Fine," I say, taking the dish rag. "But can we change the locks here, just in case?"

She nods. "Yes, absolutely. I'll call them today."

Great, I think. I just have to be alone with the random counter that held a message in the flour all day and try not to think about how weird that is. "I think I'm going to the library today," I tell her. "I want to get that card we talked about."

Her back is to me and she's almost out of the room but she pauses long enough to nod. "Fine," she says. "I'll tell the landlord he'll need to let the locksmith in himself."

After Mom leaves for work I throw some clothes on and take a drastic step, something that shows how shaken up I am by the morning. I call Ciara. Not text. Physically hit the little button that stores her contact information to dial into her phone directly.

She answers on the second ring, just as I'm getting comfortable out front on the ground. "Oh my God, who died?"

"What?" I stutter, taken off guard by her greeting. She sounds a little tired, maybe she's confused.

"You never call me. Who died?"

"Oh." I manage to squeak out a halfhearted chuckle. "No, some weird shit just happened this morning and I sort of needed a sounding board."

"Right. Gimme a second." I hear some rustling and a muffled conversation. Then a door closes and Ciara's back, sounding a lot more alert. "I only have a few. Sum it up for me."

"Sorry about taking your —" I start, assuming she's probably at work.

"We don't have time for sorry, Annie. Go."

"Right. Ok." I take a deep breath. "This morning our kitchen counter was covered in flour and someone had written DANGER in the flour on the counter," I say. "That's the fast version."

Ciara is silent for a few heartbeats. "Can you take a

picture for me?" she asks.

"I have one. Hang on." I pull my phone away from my ear and click on the picture I took before I cleaned up the mess. I push the share button and pick Ciara's text bubble. The whooshing sound is my cue to bring the phone back to my ear. "Sent," I tell her.

"Got it." Her voice is a little more distant, meaning she's now looking at the photo. "Wait, what's the EU? Does that say EU?"

"Yeah, that's what I thought it said too. I don't know what that means."

"It's not very clear," she says.

I pull the phone down again to take a second look. She's right, I notice. It's shaky and inconsistent. In fact, maybe I'm imagining it even saying DANGER. I'm sort of filling in the blanks there. That G isn't technically a G at all. More like the hint of G on the whisper of flour. The R at the end may have been a K. It's hard to tell. "Yeah, I guess it's not," I agree, putting the phone back to my ear. "But it's still creepy, right? Like I should be panicking?"

"Alright, babes, here's my thought. Nothing else in the house was touched, right?"

"Right," I agree.

"And you heard nothing?"

"Nothing."

"Mmmhmm so this was a random flour situation."

"It appears that way," I say.

"Yeah, you have to let this go," she says.

"What? Ciara, seriously, the flour didn't spill itself on

the counter and it certainly didn't —"

"Annie, you have to let it go," she interrupts. "There are no answers I can give you right this second that will make you happy. Instead, we have a whole lot of what the hell is going on and it's just too much right now. The noises stopped. This started. It's fucking weird but you have to let it go for this second."

I sigh because I don't like this idea but I'm not sure how to tell her she's wrong.

"Here's the plan. I'm going to stay over there at the new place tomorrow because I'm off the next day. I'm taking an Uber up there after work —"

I make a sound of protest because Uber's are expensive.

"—which you're paying for half of." She shuts up my protest with a solid comeback. "We're gonna drink a ton of coffee and eat a bunch of chocolate. We're gonna stay up all night waiting for whatever freaky flour writing thing decides to comes to pay you a visit. I'm telling you to let this go for right now so I can get back to work. But I'm also telling you that the night after next we're taking care of this once and for all. You with me?"

I'm not entirely sure how my body can feel like dancing and crying all at the same time, but Ciara has done it. "I fucking love you," I tell her. "You're the absolute best and I'm paying for that entire Uber."

"I was hoping you'd say that," she says. "I gotta go but I love you girlie. We're gonna figure this shit out, ok?"

"Yeah, ok. Bye for now."

"Bye for now," she echoes.

I pull my phone away when I hear her click off. I wipe the tears leaking out of the corners of my eyes, which might be happy tears at this point, and shove my phone back in my pocket. We're gonna figure this out. I feel better already.

Chapter 17

New plan in hand, I let myself drop back into the house long enough to get a water bottle and my camera bag. I spare one glance for the now clean counter before shutting the kitchen light off and turning my back on it. We may have a plan, but I don't need to sit here obsessing all day.

Instead, I'm hitting the library and then finding someplace to take pictures.

The library card turns out to be surprisingly easy to obtain, as promised. It takes me about five minutes and I only have to talk to one person behind the desk. That person even holds out two books in my direction. "These also have your name on them," she tells me.

One is a small book simply titled *AVONDALE*. The other looks more interesting. It's a larger paperback titled *It Happened in Arizona*. I pick that one up and look through it. It looks like a newspaper-style book, detailing stories and headlines from Arizona's past. "I like this one," I tell her, "but it won't fit in my camera case and I didn't bring another bag."

"It's fine," she says. "I can hold it for up to a week. Do you just want to come back tomorrow and grab it?"

"Perfect." I put both books back on the counter

between us. "Can you hold both?"

"Absolutely. We'll see you tomorrow."

I pocket my new library card and head out. The lighting in this library is gorgeous but I'm not sure they'd let me shoot here and right now my shutter finger is itching to get to work.

I walk for about five minutes before I find a cute little grassy area that grabs my attention. It takes me a surprisingly long time, and by that I may only mean five minutes, to notice the other photographer in the little park. It takes me much less time, maybe 30 seconds, to figure out that someone is Ali from the neighborhood. She's shooting with a Nikon and using a wider lens than I plan to use. "Hey." I greet her when I'm close enough not to shock her by talking.

She turns around, blinks a few times to try and place my face, and smiles. "Hey new girl, are you shooting today?" Her head tips toward my camera case.

"Hopefully," I tell her. "I got a new macro lens from my Dad. I'm trying to take it for a test drive."

"I'm looking for a good landscape shot. My mom is big into fancy calendars and I'm trying to get one put together for her birthday." She looks down at the screen of the camera where the picture she just took must be displayed. "I don't have a good appreciate-the-sunshine-in-Phoenix shot yet," she says.

"Mind if I hang near you?" I know it's ridiculous. She's taking wide lens scenery shots of the sky and I'm looking at macro stuff. But we both know photography is a solo thing, sometimes the best you can do is have someone nearby.

"Absolutely," Ali answers. "There's a nest in that

saguaro over there that may give you something," she offers.

I throw my gaze to the left, the direction she pointed, while I'm trying to free my lens from the case.

She's right. In the crook where an arm of the big cactus meets the main stalk, there's a mess of twigs and leaves. Currently, there's no bird that I can see, but maybe if I'm patient one will come back.

I get the lens fitted into the camera and stroll a few steps away from Ali to frame a shot. I'm not sure how much time goes by but eventually a bird lands. The shot I get of the wings out for a landing is amazing. I put the camera down, stretch my arms, and look for Ali. She hasn't moved far at all and is lying in the grass on her belly with her camera propped on her elbows. I try to bend down and see the angle she's coming from. Gorgeous shot of the edges of the sun's rays reaching for tree tops. I wait until I hear her shutter click a few times. "That looks awesome," I tell her.

She rolls over on her back and smiles at me. "Hey, thanks. I think I got what I wanted this time." She holds her camera in front of her face. "Smile," she says. I don't have any time to react before she hits the shutter.

"You had way too wide of a lens for that." I laugh. "Which is the only reason I won't immediately demand you delete it."

"Bet it's blurry and chaotic," she agrees. I can hear the laugh she's not letting out. "Hey, what time is it?"

I pull my phone out of my pocket and check the time. When I hold my phone out to her so she can see it, Ali jumps to her feet in one impressively smooth movement. "Shit, I have to get home. My Dad will be home from work in like thirty minutes and he'll flip his head if I'm not there."

"I should probably go too," I tell her. "I'll see you soon."

"Yeah, text me," Ali says. She's tossing stuff quickly into a camera bag that is roughly the same size as mine. "We'll hang."

Over Ali's shoulder, I notice a familiar head of hair. "Hey, isn't that the Tony guy from the neighborhood?" I ask her.

She turns, looks quickly, and turns right back to me. "Yeah, that's him. He's always hanging around. That guy he's talking to is trouble though. If that guy offers you anything, you say no." She points her finger at me. "Got it?"

"Yeah, sure." I want to know what kind of something he might offer, but I'm afraid to seem too eager. If this neighborhood is anything like the old one, she likely just means drugs anyway. Drugs are not really my thing. I wonder for a second if they're Tony's thing before I decide it's not really my business to wonder such things about some stranger from the neighborhood.

Tony looks up for just a second, his eyes landing on us. Then I see him do a double-take, letting his eyes linger longer like he's recognized one or both of us. I wave and he immediately looks away. That makes me feel like an idiot. It was probably Ali he recognized, not me.

Ali finishes zipping her camera bag and throws it over her shoulder. "Alright new girl, text me."

"I will," I tell her. As I watch her jog away toward the

neighborhood I wonder if I actually will. I decide I'll try to bring myself to do it. Maybe even when Ciara is hanging around tomorrow night. I can make friends in this neighborhood. Nothing is stopping me but myself.

Chapter 18

I get home before Mom and manage to throw some frozen chicken in the oven so we can eat. My eyes keep tracking to the counter as if I'm expecting something else unusual to happen. When it doesn't, I notice myself calming down and relaxing as the sun sets. Maybe this is all in my head. I let myself make a list of things that I can look forward to.

1. Tomorrow I'll head back to the library and pick up the books I put on hold.

2. Then I'll come back here and edit the pictures I've been taking to see if I have any decent ones. Maybe I'll even send one to Dad as a way to thank him for the lens.

3. I'll take a short nap after lunch so I'm well rested before Ciara's Uber shows up.

That makes me take a calming breath for the first time all day. Tomorrow is shaping up to be the most normal day I've had all summer. Maybe I'm settling in here. Everything is going to be fine.

"I'm home." I hear Mom call from the doorway.

I'm standing over the oven, checking the temperature of the chicken with a meat thermometer. "In here," I call back. "I made food."

"That is what I smell." She arrives in the doorway looking exhausted and maybe even a little worried. For a heartbeat, I forget why she might look like that until I notice her eyes flit nervously to that counter.

The memories come back but I shake them off. "I got my library card today," I tell her. I make sure to use my chipper voice, something normal to show her that I'm perfectly fine. I push the oven door shut, the chicken needs a few more minutes. "Also, I called Ciara this morning and she wants to come by tomorrow night and spend the night here. She'd like to check out the new place. I figured that would be fine."

"It's completely fine." Mom crosses the kitchen and brushes a kiss on my forehead before reaching for a wine glass from the cabinet behind me. "Ciara is always welcome here, you two both know that."

"That's what I figured. Probably five minutes until dinner," I say. "You have time to change if you want."

"I think I'll take you up on that. I'm changing out of these clothes and then I'll be back. Don't set the table, we'll just fill our plates right here at the counter and walk over to the table." She winks at me like this is the largest act of rebellion in the history of rebellions. I try not to laugh.

Mom and I have a nice evening at home, both succeeding in not mentioning the flour incident or the weird noises. Eventually, I even take myself to bed when my eyes are starting to close on their own. I leave my bedroom door open and the light from the bathroom on, spilling into the hallway like a scared toddler. Mom notices it but she doesn't flick it off.

I'm asleep quickly.

The peaceful evening shatters when my eyes fly open in the middle of the night. My pulse is already racing and a bad feeling sours my stomach. I don't even get a peaceful second to ponder why I'm awake before the knocking comes again.

My heartbeat slows and I breathe easily. Which seems like an odd reaction to late-night noise. But the thing is, this one is different, and different is amazing. This noise is not coming from the empty unit. It's not coming from inside our unit. It's just a light tapping on my exterior wall, the one on the opposite side of the house.

I shove my feet in my sandals and shuffle through the house. I check the windows as I pass them but see nothing in the dim light of the city at midnight. At the back door, I pause and look out along the yard for a long time. Nothing moves and the tapping is very quiet here. I push open our back door and look around. The empty unit looks completely undisturbed, which makes me smile and gives me the courage needed to venture out into the backyard.

I walk the full length of the yard behind Mom's bedroom, finding absolutely nothing. There's a gate in the low fence on this side that is identical to the gate on the other side where I took the locksmith through the other day. I push the gate open and cross into the side-yard. Again, nothing out of the ordinary greets me here. There's a tree planted on this side of the house that has rather long branches. I suppose it's possible the tapping I heard was from a limb of the tree hitting the side of the house. I squint a little up at the branches, looking for one that is long enough to reach. It seems like a stretch, but it's possible.

I stand there for a beat, waiting. I wonder if the wind may kick up and I'll be able to see the branch tapping on the wall for myself, but nothing happens.

I decide I'm willing to accept my theory that the tree was the late-night knocker. I continue my path around the front of the house, just to do a thorough search. Up here, everything continues to look normal. The car is dark with all the doors closed. The windows of our unit have the curtains drawn mostly shut and are also dark. The windows of the neighboring unit are completely dark, as usual. I decide, just on a whim, to check out the front door of the unit next door. I don't know what compulsion pulls me to do that. It's just one of those things that your brain decides is right and then you can't ignore that decision. If I try to go to bed now, I'll stay awake thinking of all the ways someone could be opening that front door just because I forgot to just take five seconds and try the handle.

My hand closes around the metal and, for no rational reason, my heartbeat speeds up. I twist the knob, shocked that it turns in my hand. Why is this door unlocked? I push it open and total blackness fills my vision.

IN BETWEEN

chapter 19

The first thing I notice is that I am not inside the empty unit.

The second thing I notice is gray, like the color. Everything around me is gray. The walls are painted, the floor is painted, and the ceiling is painted. There are no windows. I spin around and look behind me. Whatever door I remember opening is no longer there. It's just me in this completely gray room.

The third thing I notice is that there are no lights in here and yet I can see perfectly. I can see every corner of this small room. Where am I getting the light source from? Why is this not completely dark? "Hello," I call out. I try to keep my voice down because the room is not large but still, it sort of echoes back to me.

"Annie, welcome." The voice came from behind me.

I whirl around to see a black woman about my age. Her dress is a sort of flowy material, lightly wrapping around her. It looks like a dress from another era. But on her feet, she's wearing ratty old high tops, exactly the kind of kicks kids would wear to play basketball in my old neighborhood.

I pull my eyes back to her face and smile at her. "Do I know you? Where are we?"

"Let's call this the 'in-between' for now. You're being processed as we speak." She winks at me like this is a little secret she is giving me.

"Being processed for what?"

A small laugh bounces through the room. "For your afterlife, silly."

The hair on my arms raises and it's suddenly very hard to swallow. My eyes fill with water almost immediately. "I'm …" I try that swallowing thing again, managing to move some of whatever fear is suddenly making me feel like I haven't had a drink of water in millennia. "I'm dead?"

Her features melt into a frown. "I'm afraid so, dear. You don't remember anything?"

I try. I stare at the gray-painted floor and try to remember the details. I heard a tapping on the outside of my room. I got out of bed. I walked around the house. The tree, the tree was probably tapping. I waited for the wind to blow but there was no wind so I walked around the front of the house.

My eyes snap back to her face. "The front door of the other unit. I decided to try the front door."

The flash of memory that comes next makes my arms feel instantly cold and a shiver dances down my spine. The glint of light on a metal blade, sharp pain in my chest, and blood. So much blood.

I close my eyes. "No, I don't want to remember."

Just that quickly, the memories are gone. I feel my whole body relax. "That's probably for the best, dear," she says.

I shake my head. "Who are you? What happens now?"

Her smile is back. She takes a few steps around as if something is fascinating in this room and she's preparing to give me a tour. "This is the in-between. It's where we wait for you to be processed. Your processing should be done momentarily and then you can begin your afterlife."

She sounds so cheerful and yet memories of my world, my family, suddenly feel too heavy. A sob escapes my lips and my eyes fill with tears again. "This can't be real." I flop to the floor, pull my knees up to my chest, and encapsulate them in my arms. "I can't be dead. My mother needs me right now, she doesn't have anyone else. My Dad hasn't even seen me since the divorce. I wanted a future, like a real one. Ciara," new anguish tears a hole in my chest. "Oh, Ciara. She won't handle this well." I swipe a stray hair out of my face but I don't bother wiping at the fountain of tears. There are too many waiting to take the place of whatever I wipe away. "I'm so young. I had so many plans for my future. I didn't even get to really … to really," the words sort of dissolve into tears. I'm not making sense. "It's not fair," I manage to get out.

She kneels beside me and I feel impossibly light hands rubbing circles on my back. "You're in pain."

I just nod. Because, obviously.

"Let me ask you a question." I pick my head up from where it was buried among my arms and look at her face. "Do you think you could have stopped your death?"

I nod vehemently. "Yes."

She appears to consider something, looking up at the gray ceiling. I get the impression she's listening to something but I don't hear anything. Then she stands up. The motion is fluid and graceful. She holds out her hand to me and when I slip mine inside of hers, it's warm and soft. She pulls me to my feet.

"Alright, Miss Annie, one chance. We have one way we can do this and no time to explain the rules or why they're in place. Just trust me when I say this is the only path available. One chance and the outcome is final. Are we clear?"

I squint at her. "Um, not really. Are you saying I'm not dead?"

She leans in close so I can see a little sparkle in her eyes. "I'm saying you get one do-over. Use it wisely."

She kisses me on the cheek and everything fades to black.

Part Two

chapter 20

My eyes flutter open and I stretch my arms over my head, waking up my muscles as well as my mind. Then my brain registers my surroundings. I jump to my feet. I am not in my bed at home, where I thought I would be for a split second. I'm in a dark empty room with a layer of dust on the floorboards. Panic rises in my throat. I force myself to take a deep breath. This room is not entirely gray, like the last room I remember waking up in. I shudder at that memory and pieces of the conversation I had with the beautiful woman rush through my brain. She said this is my second chance, whatever that means.

I need to figure out where I am. I look around again, taking notice of the small details. The floorboards are fake wood, I think, like the ones in my bedroom, but dirtier. There's a single window, but I cannot see out of it. I can barely see the edge of sunlight around the outside, forming a faint rectangle. I move to the window and try to pull back the thick black curtains that are blocking the sunlight. I can't. My hand passes right through them. The waves of panic swell inside me, threatening to drown me. I have to calm myself down.

I hold my hand in front of my face and stare at it. It looks fine. It looks the same as always, fingernails kept trimmed down low to make pressing buttons on my camera easier and perpetually dry skin.

I stomp my foot. I feel the ground underneath me. I feel the pressure radiate up my leg when I stomp. But there's no noise. No cloud of dust rises from the floorboards. In fact, looking around the room, I notice I didn't leave any footprints in the dust when I moved to the window.

I put my hand in front of my face again. It looks the same, but maybe I'm not solid. I move my hand closer to myself until I'm touching my nose. It feels the same. Everything feels the same. My skin feels smooth and warm. What is happening?

I hear the sound of a car door closing. It sounds like it comes from the other side of the window. I move closer to the window, squinting and trying to see through the heavy curtains.

My hand slips right through the wall.

Maybe that's the answer. I don't have to part the curtains if I can move through objects. I lean forward, deciding to commit to the motion. Like nothing was there at all, I end up on the other side. The wall I was just staring at is solidly behind me. I want to be shocked that I just did that but another shock overpowers it. This one robs everything from me: I can't move, I can't breathe. I'm just standing there like a statue, watching.

I am watching myself.

There am I, standing just outside the passenger door of Mom's new car in my comfortable yoga capri pants and loose tank top. My hair is clipped up off my neck. I'm in full I-don't-care-what-I-look-like mode because we were supposed to be driving all day. "Mom, is something wrong with this house?" the other me asks.

Oh my God. It's moving day. I'm back to moving day.

I watch in total disbelief as my Mother leads the other me through the front door of the house. I've done this before. I reach up and rub my eyes, hard. I have to try and remember what happened when I was in that gray room she kept calling the in-between. Like, the details. What did that woman say?

She said I get one chance. She said the outcome was permanent.

I don't have to die.

She also said there were rules.

I look down at my hands again. One of those rules must be that I'm not really here. I'm, what, an angel? A memory? No, that can't be right. I haven't happened yet. I'm more like a future. A shadow.

It doesn't matter what I call myself.

I turn around and look at the house. The wall I just dropped out of was not the house I'm moving into. It's the empty unit. I just came out of the bedroom that would be my bedroom if we lived in the empty unit.

I can use that unit. I know it's not in use. I can make it sort of a base. It's close to me — the other me. I can watch myself and keep anything bad from happening to me. Maybe I can reach out and try to talk to myself or something. Maybe I can get a message to myself, warn me.

I take a deep breath and look back at the house. I try to remember how many days we had lived there before everything happened. I'm finding it hard to remember the details, for some reason. Like there's a block on some of the information. I really hope it's a case of bad memory and not a case of one of those rules the lady in-between talked about. Because that seems entirely unfair.

I think it was five days. I think I have five days to try and figure out who kills me and stop them from doing it. Five days.

I hope it's enough time.

Chapter 21

I spend the day conducting little tests of my abilities in an attempt to learn more about these rules. Here's what I come up with:

1.   I cannot interact with anything. I can't lift things, I can't talk to people, I can't be seen by anyone, and I can't move things. I can walk on the floor without falling through the earth, which is good, but I can't lean on walls or sit on chairs.

2.   I can't fly. I can hover for a little while, but it's more of a slow fall from a high jump. I tried this while Annie (that's the easiest way to refer to the original version of myself, I've decided) and Mom were moving the couch. It almost made me think, for a second, that I was actually sitting on the couch. Nope, I just kept slowly floating until I ended up on the ground. So, I can't fly and I can't sit on the couch.

3.   I still don't really remember details from before. It's weird. I'm watching them happen and I remember them as a sort of deja vu but I can't remember what must come next. So, for example, as I watched Annie secretly texting Ciara from inside the moving truck she's supposed to be

getting a box from I remembered that. But I didn't remember that Mom came outside and caught her texting. I didn't remember that Mom tossed a couch pillow at her, laughing and telling her to get back to work. At least, not until I saw it happen. This is, by far, the most infuriating little rule. I'm not going to be able to remember helpful details until they happen, I think. How am I supposed to work with that?

At the end of the day when Annie and Mom head to bed, I am surprised to find that my body, if it can accurately be called a body, feels exactly the same. No fatigue, no soreness, no yawning. I'm not hungry, I don't have to pee, and my eyes aren't tired and dry. I've basically been in the same condition all day. I guess that's a positive benefit to this whole not-a-real-body thing. It means I can maximize my five-day timetable by working all night.

With that in mind, I pace back and forth in the kitchen of the formerly empty unit and try to come up with a plan. The most important part is that I obviously need to warn myself that I will die in five days. Of course, I have no idea who is going to kill me. I also have no idea how to prevent it from happening.

I stop my pacing. If this were a comic strip, a lightbulb would appear above my head, I would point my finger at the sky and yell "Eureka". Maybe I don't need to focus so much on the previous Annie. Maybe I need to try and find out what shady character decides to end my life.

Of course, what would I do to stop that? I currently

have absolutely no way of interacting with the living world.

I felt like I was on to something there, but it's not quite a full idea yet. So I resume my pacing. This entire ordeal seems a little lopsided, I decide. It's completely unfair. First, I'm put into a situation where I'm brutally murdered. Then, I'm given what seems like a way to stop it from happening but instead turns out to have this crazy set of rules with no direction. No matter how it seemed when I was standing in that gray room, this is completely unfair.

A cloud of dust floats up from the floor. I stop my pacing and look back down at the ground. There's a footprint. A clear, solid, footprint. Did I do that? No one else is on this side of the unit right now, I've checked. So that footprint came from me. How did I do that? I shouldn't be able to interact with the dust on the floor (see the list of things I have learned #1). So how did I just make a footprint?

I stomp my foot again. Nothing happens.

That makes me angry all over again because I hate that I can't understand the rules that are guiding whatever form I am in right now. I stomp my way across the room, toward the wall, and throw a fist at the refrigerator.

The first thing I notice is that my fist aches and the pain radiates up my arm. The second thing I notice is the fridge wobbles a little. I shouldn't be able to interact with anything, but I just did. Twice.

I stop and think. Both times I was angry, to a boiling point.

Can it be that simple?

Do I have to be focused on some kind of emotion? I'm

sure there's a lesson there about tapping into the emotions that make me human, but I don't spend too much time analyzing. Instead, I think of all the things that make me angry and start stomping my feet back and forth in front of the wall, testing.

I'd say about a third of the footprints make an impression and a noise. I'm excited, as weird as that seems. What else can I interact with if I can keep myself feeling something?

I keep up the experiments, trying to open cabinets around the kitchen. It takes me about seven tries, but the cabinet door finally flies open with a bang. This is a good step. I'm not consistent but maybe I can interact with things if I just keep trying. I turn my attention to shutting the cabinet. It seems like the more I get frustrated with failed attempts the easier it is to have a good attempt. As if proving my point, the cabinet slams shut on my eighth try.

I try again. Fail, fail, fail, fail, GET FRUSTRATED and then fail, fail, OPEN.

This is amazing.

I try to remember that frustrating feeling I was having before it opened. But my hand still slips right through the cabinet door. Oh yes, that frustration. Close my eyes and feel that ball of anger right at my breast bone. Ball my fist, try again. The cabinet slams closed.

I can't help myself, I feel triumphant. I let myself do what can only be described as a happy dance around the empty room. For whatever reason, happiness doesn't appear to work because nothing happens.

I stop my dance when I'm facing the wall of Annie's

unit. I take a few steps closer and consider the fridge again. I decide I'm going to try opening that, although I'm mildly afraid of what kind of smell may come out to meet me. Aren't you supposed to keep unused appliances like that propped open?

I'm facing it, trying to tap into my frustration and anger on the first try when I hear lots of noise coming from next door. My eyes pop open and I stare at the wall, trying to remember.

There's banging and boxes shuffling. The memory comes back. Annie is in the kitchen, looking for a snack. I rush the wall, letting myself float right through it and there I am. I'm holding a box of cheese crackers. The memory keeps coming. I was in the kitchen because I heard a noise. I turn and look at the unit behind me and the realization feels like ice water. The noise was me. Is that possible?

Annie takes her cheese snacks, flips the light off, and leaves the room. My eyes adjust to the darkness rather quickly and I wait in silence before trying anything new. I don't want to disturb Annie again. I need to be more careful.

When it seems like it's been a long time, although I suppose I can't judge anymore, I start my experiments again. I'm able to move chairs in and out, flip on the light, turn on the coffee pot, turn on the faucet, and open the fridge. I keep practicing until I can do those things on command every other time I try.

I'm feeling proud of myself until I hear a noise coming from the other end of the house. I turn and look out the window. The sky is still dark but it's lightening. I've been practicing all night. Again, I'm shocked that I feel no different even after working hard all night long. I shake it off as the noise from the other end of the house gets louder. Mom is awake and moving around. I hear her bedroom door open and footsteps headed my way.

I turn my attention to the chair I'd just pulled out, trying to push it back in. But to get it on an early try, I have to focus on my feelings of frustration and right now all I'm feeling is panic. My first seven attempts result in the chair staying in the same spot.

I hear the bathroom toilet flush. The familiar frustration builds and the chair slides into place. My shoulders sag with relief. I hear Mom's footsteps drawing closer so I take a last look around the room, making sure everything is back to where it belongs. The light. I left the light on in the room the last time I turned it on. It was easier to see. I quickly race across the room and focus on trying to turn it off.

My first pass goes right through the wall and the switch and I realize that's probably a good thing. She's close enough now that she would've seen the light go out. That would draw more attention, not less. I decide to leave it like it is. That's when the memory comes back. Mom thinks this one is Annie. I remember her asking about it, asking if I left it on.

I squint at the switch in confusion. Small memories are starting to drop into place yet instead of making me feel more comfortable they're making me more confused. How is it possible that I'm doing these things now that line up with the past?

My brain hurts from thinking about it. Mom is just outside the room when I am backing through the wall.

Something in my memory tugs at my brain and forces me to look at the fridge.

I'm not even surprised when I notice I left it slightly ajar.

chapter 22

The smell of cinnamon wafts into the empty unit shortly after Mom has scared me back over here and that's when I decide I can't stay here all day. I remember the cinnamon bread and I can't torture myself by smelling it without being able to taste it. My stomach doesn't even rumble as it should in response to the smell. Completely unfair.

I walk through the back wall of the house, straight across the back yard, through our fence, and into another yard. I don't really know where I'm going so I just keep walking in a straight line until I'm standing on the street behind us that runs parallel to ours. This far away from the original Annie and her day that comes back to me when I see it happen, I can focus on what needs to be done. I need to find whoever it is that decides to end my life. I just need a plan.

Looking up and down the street I spy one person out of their house at this hour on a weekend. Someone is getting into a car. I move closer, trying to see details of the person. The pixie cut jogs my memory. Ali, I think her name is. I remember the conversation, photography club, and the yearbook. She's wearing the same outfit, I notice. The same earrings. Is that today? Does Annie meet this girl today? I actually remember the car too, I realize. This car is the one they're all leaning on when I take my walk and see them.

The memory is fuzzy and distant. It's like trying to remember an intense dream you had three days after you had it. I decide that means it hasn't happened yet. Annie hasn't met this girl and her friends hanging out by this car. Judging by the outfit, that's happening later today.

Ali turns on her car, messes with the radio, and then drives off. I stand in the street watching her drive away trying to figure out if I just broke a rule about memory by knowing who this girl was before past me has even met her.

A few houses down, someone slides out from underneath a car parked in a different driveway. The movement pulls my attention out of my own head. The guy, who I can only tell from this distance away is skinny and scruffy, rubs his hands on his pants, and walks up to the front door of the house. He knocks on the door and shoves his hands in his back pockets to wait. I decide to head that way and see what's going on.

When I get to the house, he's having a discussion with whoever answered the door. I can't hear them, but there's a lot of gesturing to the car. The person inside the house smiles, and offers his hand. The other guy shakes it, nodding. A $20 bill gets pulled out of a pocket and handed to the guy outside. Then the door is closing and the guy turns to head my way.

I recognize him too, I realize. Memories come back. The guy leaning on the car told me his name is Tony. Or he will tell me. Whatever. He also told me Tony fixes cars. Then I saw Tony again, I think. I wrack my brain trying to access that fuzzy memory. I remember with a quick flash, like a scene from a movie played behind my eyelids for just a second. I saw him at the library and in a park.

Ok, so this memory thing isn't completely flawed, apparently. I can remember things when they're relevant. So this is relevant right now. I remember his name and I remember the neighborhood people called him a "nice guy".

A quick look in both directions reveals no one else on the street. Tony isn't jumping in a car, he's walking. That means there's no one else around and I can probably keep up with his pace so I decide to follow Tony. Maybe he'll lead me somewhere interesting, with more people around. He's walking fast in the direction of the main road. I have to run to keep up with him. In case you were wondering, it is really weird to run without feeling the normal consequences of running. My legs aren't tired, my muscles aren't screaming at me, and I don't have to breathe heavily. Weird.

At the main road, Tony takes a right then he takes a left at the first intersection. I follow him through the intersection and look around. There's a convenience store ahead of us, the red and white banner commonplace all over the valley. The parking lot is pretty empty at this time of the morning. But just to the right of the store is an overpass for a busier street. Underneath that, there's a gathering of people. People are what I was in search of so when Tony pops into a convenience store, I keep walking.

I have to be honest, if I were completely normal, I would probably avoid heading toward these people. They look a little sketchy, standing underneath an overpass. But I figure in this form they can't hurt me. Plus if I'm trying to find someone who may kill me, isn't sketchy something I should be paying attention to?

The closer I come to the people the more detail comes into focus, like turning the lens on my camera. Some are smoking, some are holding bottles wrapped in brown paper bags which I thought people only did in movies. A few of them are sleeping up against the pillars for the overpass. There's a shopping cart full of something with a coat draped over it and a little dog who needs a bath shaking in the corner. It's too hot out for this dog to be cold. I wonder if the shaking is an indication of some health problem, but I can't be sure. The people are just as much of a mystery. Their ages are hard to make out. They could be my age, buried under the clothing and the grime, or they could be the age of my parents. Living like this would age you.

Sadness sort of floods into me. I just left a home with electricity and water and these people are sleeping like this. Of course, I know there are homeless people in the world. I guess in my sheltered life, I just never met anyone who lived that way. Standing here watching these people, I can't help but feel like this is a problem that needs more attention.

I drop cross-legged onto the ground, watching. Suddenly, it seems more important to figure out a way I can help here, even if it's only a small thing. But I have no clue how I can be of service. I can barely even interact with the world.

"Anyone want a hot dog?" a voice calls out.

I stand up and turn, facing the sound. Tony is holding a plastic bag from the convenience store packed with silver-

silver-wrapped packages. I squint at him, this boy who fixes cars and wanders my neighborhood. I watch him hand out hot dogs to everyone under the overpass. He even slips one to the sad-looking dog. I don't count how many there are, but he has a few left after everyone has one.

"I don't need all these," he says. "I'm just going to leave the bag."

"Thanks, Tony," someone says.

"Don't mention it. Honestly, they gave them to me cheap because no one else was even considering hot dogs this early in the morning." He rakes his hand back up through his hair and drops the bag on the ground. "Don't let them go to waste, alright?"

"Yeah, we won't. Thanks, man." The man steps a little closer to Tony and drops his voice. I lean in to listen. "Do you need anything, kid?"

Tony shakes his head. "I'm alright. I'll be alright."

"I heard about the job, though. You got someplace to stay?"

Tony nods. "Yeah, I'm staying with my father for now."

The man closes his eyes and shakes his head. "That's not the best idea, kid. Sometimes the price is worth paying, you know what I mean?"

I don't know about Tony, but I know I have no idea what that means.

Tony frowns. "It's temporary." He pats the man's shoulder. "I'll be alright." Then he turns up his voice and, once again, addresses the whole group. "I gotta run, but you guys take it easy. Be safe."

I stand there watching the group for a little while, wondering how much more there is about the world I didn't understand before I died. I have spent my entire life sheltered away from all of this. This is real life, right here under this overpass eating hot dogs because there's nothing else to eat and yet worrying about the neighborhood kid not having a place to stay.

I decide, right then, that I have to change something. I have to find a way to change my future so I can be a better citizen. Why didn't I ever bring a bag of hot dogs to people who have no food? Why didn't I ever ask Tony if he had a place to stay? Why didn't I help anyone, ever?

I have to find a way to survive because I have a lot of being-a-better-person things to do. Starting now.

Chapter 23

I spend the rest of the sunlit hours checking out other areas around town. Besides the apparently homeless group under the overpass near the convenience store, I find other groups of people. I find a bunch of people playing basketball on the courts outside the high school even though it is summer and the high school is closed. There are a couple of kids smoking something on the handball courts at the high school too, but they might be from the same group. There's a funeral home that was packed with cars today. I didn't spend a lot of time there because that made me sad. My parents might need that funeral home if I can't figure this whole puzzle out.

Then I found a little park that I sort of remember from before. It has that same random memory feel as Ali and Tony like it's something I'm aware of but Annie isn't. The park is exactly like the parks near the old house, which is to say it's a lot of grass and large trees that look entirely unnatural in this particular desert environment. In the center of the park is a large man-made watering hole of some kind. Clearly, it was meant to be the focal point, a sort of "look, we have water here" statement. It doesn't smell the best and it seems to be swarming with some kind of tiny flying bug. I wouldn't swim in it, is what I'm saying.

I walk around the park for a bit, paying attention to the people around here. I'm looking for suspicious characters but, honestly, I don't even know what that really means. It would be more helpful if the person who was going to kill me would just walk around in a large white hockey mask or wear claws for fingers.

As a side note, I'm starting to think animals can see me. The ducks at the park sort of followed me around for about half an hour when I first got here. Then a little kid ran at them trying to pet one and they didn't bother me again. But it made me wonder. Is it all animals, just birds, or just ducks?

If you had asked me before today about homeless people, I would have guessed you'd find them at a park. I think that's because I associate green trees with comfort. I'd want to hang out under a tree in a grassy area if I had nowhere else to go. Now I know that's not the case. I found families, teenagers, and people who work at the park cleaning up. But that's about it.

As far as questionable people who may end up killing me go, I strike out completely. I keep thinking it will be obvious, like a part of me will know exactly who it is when I see them. But, I got nothing. I'm trying to find the answer. I'm watching every person I pass for signs of something dangerous or deadly. That's how this works in movies, right? You find that person and you can see it in their eyes that they're dangerous. How do we find these people in real life?

When night falls in the park, I head back to the house. I'm frustrated, stressed, and completely at a loss for what to do next. At the driveway, I stand there and stare at the house. Annie's side, the left side, is dark because my entire life is asleep in there. The right side is dark because it's empty. I frown at the house. Something about that empty right side is tugging and pulling at me, but I can't latch onto the memory.

I don't close my eyes. I stare at the front door, willing my brain to cooperate. A flash of memory dances across my eyes, dripping red blood and a lot of pain. Then it's gone.

That door triggered my memory flash. That side of the house. Is that where the danger is? Do I need to keep Annie out of that side of the house?

I step closer to the empty unit and lay my hand on the front door. Of course, I can't feel the wood or the heat of the summer day we've just had. My hand goes right through to the other side. Frustrated, I pull my hand back out and stare at the door. "I want to remember just a little," I say. "Just enough to be able to help."

This time the flash is more shocking, if not more helpful. Pain, blood, and the glint of light on a blade. It's gone in a blink but I definitely had that memory. That's the answer. Something on this side of the house is dangerous. I have to keep Annie out of this unit.

I rush back across the lawn and walk through the front door of Annie's house. I pause in the entryway and look around, trying to find some way I can get a message to my past self. My eyes fall on the far wall and the bookshelf. The memory comes back, Annie and Mom set up the bookshelf today.

Maybe books are the answer, I realize. Books are how

Annie communicates. She'll pass a book she loves to someone because she knows it will say things to them that she isn't ready or can't say. Books are her magic.

Maybe I can't directly talk to Annie, but I can get her a message. I'll use books.

I hover my finger along the shelves, reading spines and looking for titles that might give off the right message. My eyes land on a Tom Clancy book, *Clear and Present Danger*. That one seems a little obvious, but it might work. I glance at each title and return to the beginning, trying to find something better. Mary Burton's *You're Not Safe* draws my attention next. Yes, that's better. But not specific enough. James Patterson's *The House Next Door* seems a little too vague, doesn't it? But what if I can pull them all together? What if I can find something to connect them all in a way that makes sense to Annie? A completely clear message.

My eyes land on RL Stine's *Stay Out of the Basement* spine and suddenly, it's completely clear.

I stand with my eyes closed, focusing my energy and trying to connect. I'll only get one really good shot at this. I have to do it right. It takes three tries to get down the first book, but the rest come on the first try. I drop them to the floor with audible thumps and then organize them carefully.

I overlap the Patterson title to cover the end of the RL Stine title. Then I pull back to look at what I've done. I don't have much time to appreciate it before I see the flashlight beam start to bounce around in the hallway. Forgetting that Annie can't see me, I pull back out of the way and up against the far wall.

I hope she sees the message.

Clear and Present Danger. You're Not Safe. Stay Out of The House Next Door.

I know that's how it reads if you look at the titles. I mumble the phrases over and over again as if that act can help her to understand. I watch her reach like she's going to clean them up. Then she backs up again. She looks at the shelf, she looks confused.

I think it's working. She understands this couldn't be an accident.

She takes a picture and, instantly, I feel better. Because that means she doesn't have to get the message right this second. She can look at that picture later and figure it out. That's the best solution I could've hoped for.

Annie collects the books and slides them neatly back into their places on the bookshelf and the memory takes my breath away. I remember that picture. I remember taking it.

I also remember never looking at it again.

chapter 24

After the frustrating experience of trying to communicate messages to myself through book covers, I spend the rest of the night pacing the empty unit trying to come up with a better plan. I can't come up with anything. What I do notice is that I cannot stay at the house any longer. I am accomplishing absolutely nothing there. I decide a change of scenery, out among people, might be a better plan.

That's when I remember the high school. There were people there when I was exploring. I'm not the kind of person you'd find hanging out at a high school during the summer. I'm not the kind of person you'd find playing basketball outdoors during the heat of a desert summer. Of course, I'm also not the kind of person who would murder someone. I guess that means I need to find people who are not like me. Where better to do that than somewhere I would never be?

So I head to the high school and wait.

By the time the sun comes up, I've walked the entire campus already and am back at the basketball court. The concrete includes four full courts, which means eight hoops are forming two parallel lines like little soldiers awaiting orders. Behind one set of soldiers, there's a chain link fence with a gate that latches but doesn't lock. On the other side, there are four concrete cubicles for handball. All of those are currently as empty as the basketball court. But I remember when I was here yesterday—I think it was yesterday—there were people here. Maybe they'll come back today. I can wait.

I pace around, reconsidering my plan as doubt trickles in. It's funny how you can't appreciate time passing in this form. If you don't get tired, thirsty, hungry, have to pee, or need to sit, does time really pass?

The answer is yes, it does. I know that because I see my shadow shifting across the concrete as the sun moves across the sky. But if it wasn't for the sun, I wouldn't be sure. I never realized before how much humans rely on their bodies to tell them time has passed. I groan and throw my head back when I realize I just thought of myself as something OTHER than human. Then, for good measure, I let out a scream that no one can hear. It makes me feel better if nothing else.

After what feels like long enough, judging by the position of the sun in the sky, I take another lap around the large campus. About halfway through my walk, I realize that this is the outdoor campus where I will have my Senior year if things go right. That makes me slow down a bit and appreciate what I'm looking at. Cafeteria, gymnasium, and buildings labeled 100, 200, 300, and 400. I wish I knew what those numbers meant. Is it like the 200 building is for Math? In that case, why not helpfully label it MATH? I guess it probably corresponds to a room number. I can almost imagine the little black numbers printed out on the screen telling me where I would have my class. I let myself get lost in the daydream of seeing *Advanced Digital Photography-Room 307*. I don't know why that room number comes to me. It just feels right. I actually stand outside the 300 building, wondering if I should walk through the walls and investigate.

In the end, I don't. Because a locked door may not keep me out but it will keep out anyone I should be focused on investigating right now and that's basically the same thing. I finish my loop of the school and end up back on the courts. But this time, I'm not alone.

Two cars have parked in the little lot adjacent to the court. The gate is unlatched and standing open. Seven boys and one girl are on the court, immersed in what appears to be a game. Four of the boys have their shirts off, chests glistening in the sun. The rest, including the girl, are wearing shirts. Well, technically, the girl is wearing a sports bra that my mother would say is not appropriate outerwear, but I assume that counts.

My current status means I don't have to worry about people running into me. So I take full advantage of this and move onto the court to get a better look. Guy 1 looks intense. He's on the no-shirt team. He is the kind of guy who takes running to the hoop in a pickup game way too seriously. I also notice he's the only white guy out here. I make a mental note to remember this guy, he just seems too aggressive for my liking.

Guy 2, also of the skins, keeps laughing at everything. He has this high-pitched obnoxious laugh that sort of grates on my nerves. I notice that it seems to grate on Guy 3's nerves too. He's on the shirts team and he appears to be intentionally fouling Guy 2 shortly after some of these laughing fits. Guy 4 calls him out for it every time. Alright, so I decide, of these four, I need to keep my eye on Guy 1-Aggressive and Guy 3-Possible vigilante. Mentally noted.

Guys 5 and 6 almost look like they wandered into this basketball game by accident. They're not really running, even when it seems like the play would call for it. Maybe they're just acquaintances who were dragged in to even out teams? That idea sort of makes sense, since they're on two different teams. I decide to dismiss them from my mental notes. They remind me of puppies. Totally harmless puppies who follow their owners everywhere.

Guy 7 is the tallest and most muscular guy out here. He's the last member of the skins team and, honestly, he looks like he belongs in a movie more than on this court with a bunch of people my age. I stand right in front of him, watching him dribble all the way down the court. Guy 6 sort of makes a halfhearted attempt to block him, holding his arm out, but he easily dodges that. He gets to the other end and makes a basket, easily. No one else stood a chance of stopping him. This guy is quite the athletic specimen. Should that warrant putting him on the list? I decide it's not enough on its own. Plus, he sort of has a kind smile.

Lastly, the only girl. I'm trying to size her up and figure out if she's a threat when the game stops. "Enough of a beating for me," Guy 5 says. "I'm smoking this joint. Who's with me?"

Guy 1 groans. "You promised you'd play a full game."

"I lied." Guy 5 holds up what I assume is a joint based on about a hundred movies. "Joint?" he asks again. When no one answers, he shrugs. "Suit yourselves." Then he heads for the concrete handball cubicles.

"We'll have uneven teams now, dickwad," Guy 1 shouts. I decide to mentally cross this guy off my list. Aggressive, yes. But if dickwad is the best you can come up with, are you really that dangerous? Plus, he's clearly unhappy with this friend but he's not approaching him or getting violent. Why would he randomly get violent with some girl from the neighborhood he's never met? Isn't basketball worth fighting over more than … whatever the heck I might have done?

"I'll join him, then you'll be even," Girl offers.

"Typical," Guy 1 groans. Then he holds his hands out in front of him like he's holding an imaginary basketball. "What the fuck ever. Pass me the ball, let's do this."

The game resumes but I follow the pairing who left. After all, I still have this girl to figure out. She's taller than me and more athletic than me. Something about her face looks kind, though. Years of being around girls of all personality types have taught me what kind looks like. This girl doesn't look like the type of girl who will spread a rumor about you around campus, is what I'm saying.

They drop beside each other on the concrete and Guy lights the joint. Each of them takes a long drag, blowing the smoke up toward the sky. Then he puts the joint down on the floor and she climbs in his lap, wrapping her arms around his neck. I slip out of the cubicle before the serious making-out gets started because, honestly, that seems a little too voyeuristic for my tastes. I have to walk further away than I think I will because, it turns out, the sound of two people heavily making out on a handball court echoes.

I watch the rest of the game, noting nothing else out of the ordinary. Eventually, 5 and 8 rejoin the group, just to sit on the sidelines and watch. I continue to have exactly one suspect here, Guy 3. I still haven't heard anyone else use his name. The closest I got is Guy 4 calling him "Asshole" when he fouled him even though they're on the same team. I decide he's exactly what I'm looking for: intense, easily angered, and willing to become physical if pushed. This is why I decide to follow him to the small car he's riding in when they're finished with the game.

New dilemma, if I can't interact with things how am I supposed to tag along with a car? I jump up on the back, figuring I'll try to hold onto the trunk lid or something. Instead, I fall right through it, slowly. I get a pretty cool view of the dark trunk on my way through and then I'm on the ground underneath the car. So, that didn't work.

I try again, this time focusing my energy. I make a loud thump on the trunk lid, which causes the entire group to spin in my direction. That makes me nervous, which makes me forget what I was focusing on, which leads me to fall right through until I'm staring up at the ground again.

The car starts and I make a dive toward the window. I'm hoping I'll be translucent enough to get through the door and then become sort of solid and land on the laps of the people in the back.

Mid-air I realize this plan has a major fault. Namely, if I'm solid enough to stay on their laps won't they feel me there? I have no clue, since I've never tried to interact with an actual person in the way I interacted with cabinets and appliances back at Annie's.

I sail through the door just as the car reverses. Then I sail right through the people. When I say people, I mean all of them. Because I fall so slowly that the car reverses right through me. So, they pop the car into drive and I'm still in the parking space. Frustrated and definitely not following the car.

I lay on the ground in the spot the car was previously in watching it drive away. I have no idea where that car full of people was going. I have no way of following that guy or finding him again later. I don't even know his name.

This means my best plan so far, the one I spent pretty much an entire day on, just failed.

I need a new plan.

I stand up and start walking. I'm going to die if I can't figure out who kills me and how to stop them from doing it but I'm making absolutely no progress. None.

Frustration trickles through and I let myself feel it. This is so unfair. I'm not walking in a particular direction, just sort of stomping my way away from the high school thinking about how completely unfair this is. Sure, whoever I met in the unhelpfully named in between saw fit to give me a second chance. But can this really be called a second chance? I'm not back on earth as Annie getting to relive this whole day. I'm not even here to interact and change anything. I have absolutely no idea what I'm —

I stop in the middle of the sidewalk because something just occurred to me. I was making noise. I turn and look behind me, checking for other people. No one is on the sidewalk right now. Other than cars driving by on the street, I'm alone.

So who was making that stomping?

I had to be me. That just confirms that when I'm angry or frustrated I'm more solid. I have no idea how I can use this to my advantage. I look around again, my eyes sweeping past the cars and the businesses lining the sidewalk. I notice I've been unconsciously headed back to Annie's house and the empty unit.

Of course I was. This place is like a base. When I have nowhere else to go, I'll keep defaulting right back here.

I finish the route and float through the front entrance of the empty unit, intent on angrily practicing my ability to interact with the world until I'm confident I can land on that trunk lid and stay there. A noise at the back of the house grabs my attention and makes me freeze.

What the —

"I'm going to open this door because I smell smoke," I hear someone yell in Mom's voice.

The memory comes back when I hear someone tinkering with the door handle.

Mom. Picked. That. Lock. I try to remember what day that happened. Is it today? Is this the day she came through the door during dinner?

The back door pushes open and Mom's face is in the doorway. "Hey," I yell. I put all my anger and passion into the yell. I have no idea if this will do anything, but I have to try. "Hey, I'm right here. I'm warning you. You have to help me. I die! Someone is going to kill me and I have to figure out who it is. I need your help."

Mom steps fully into the room, Annie right behind her.

For my part, I wave my arms around like a lunatic, shouting at the top of my voice about death and warnings. I'm not fully paying attention to the words I'm saying, I'm more focused on trying to match that feeling I have before I interact with the environment.

No emotion is registering on Mom's face. I want to see shock, fear, anger, something. But I get blank eyes and a face that looks resigned. She's not hearing me. I walk closer, really get in her face. "Mom, please," I whisper. "You have to help me. I'm so scared."

"It's not impossible, Annie. No one lives here," she says. Her mouth keeps moving, but I stop listening. Because that's my answer. She didn't hear me. She can't hear me. I'm alone.

chapter 25

Review of the things I've learned.

1.   I can interact with the environment if I'm angry or frustrated, but apparently, that doesn't extend to my vocal cords.

2.   I don't get tired or have any other wear normal to human bodies.

3.   I have exactly one suspect, Aggressive Guy 3 from basketball. But unless I figure out how to get in or on a car, I'm not following him home to further investigate.

4.   There's a whole world of people hurting out there that I never did anything to help. People who need me to survive this so I can be a better person for them.

That's a pathetic list. I take a stroll around the neighborhood, which is perfectly dark and boring at this time of the night. I head out toward the area where I saw the people sleeping under the overpass and I'm not surprised to find them still there. In fact, there are actually more people here right now than there were earlier. They are curled up on sleeping bags or standing around a small camping lantern. In the movies, you always see a fire in a trash can, but there's no trash can here. Of course, I can assume that's because it's really hot and dry here so a fire would be a bad idea. I assume the heat is also why a few people are on sleeping bags but no one is actually in them. I watch for a while, although I honestly don't know how long. I listen to conversations about areas of town that are safe, someone kind who shared a meal, and a panhandling location that works.

Then, because most of the people are now laying down to sleep, I leave. I have nowhere else to go, no other bright ideas, so I just head back to Annie's house.

First I check on Mom. She's sleeping peacefully on her side, her arm curled underneath her pillow. The urge to hug her is suddenly very strong. I kneel, putting my face right next to hers. I can't sit on the bed, but this is the closest I can get. "Mom, I'm really scared," I tell her. I don't bother whispering because she won't be able to hear me anyway. "I have to figure out what happened or things will be so hard for you and Dad. I mean, they're already hard but this wouldn't help. I don't know what I'm doing, Mom. But I'm trying." I lean closer to her, feeling the tears build up in my throat. I try to press my lips to her cheek, really focusing on the emotion I'm feeling. I feel them sort of brushing her and the contact makes the tears drip right down my cheek. "I'm not giving up, I promise."

Then, before I can really fall apart and get emotional I check on Annie. I find her asleep on the kitchen table, her legs crossed and her arm holding up her head.

The memory of this one is a little hazy. I think I remember coming out to sleep on this table because I thought there would be a noise. I can't remember if I heard one. Back through the wall I go. I decide I don't want to remember anyway. That would mean I was letting her actions, which are really my actions, dictate my current actions. That makes my head hurt, it's too much to think about.

I hear a noise out back and decide to go check it out. I'm expecting wind or an animal of some kind. So I'm shocked when it's a person. An actual person walking up the side of the house and around the back here. I stand still, frozen in shock, and the person walks right through me to the back door.

I spin around and watch as this person crouches down at the handle like they know what they are doing. Just like Mom did when I watched her pick the lock. I get closer, really get in the face. Underneath the black hood of the sweatshirt which is totally conspicuous in a Phoenix summer, the face is masculine.

He gets the lock to pop open and slips through the door, shutting it behind him. Nope, you're not keeping me out that easily. I follow him through the door. I'm feeling a sense of panic right now. It's not the same as panic when you're a normal human person. I can't feel my heartbeat speeding up or the change in the temperature of my skin. I just feel a serious sense of urgency. This is happening. This person is here, right now.

He looks around the kitchen and then heads off in the direction of the living room. I stand right there, on the other side of the wall from where Annie is sleeping, and focus my energy. I tap urgently on the wall, like a knock. I'd say one in every fourth knock gets through, which has to be enough. I can hope.

Then I follow the guy. He's now in the bathroom area but before I can even get in there to see what he's doing, he comes back out and pulls that door shut like whatever he found doesn't interest him. He moves into the back bedroom, the one that would be Mom's if we were in the occupied unit. He nods a little to himself as he looks around, then he pulls his hood off.

My breath catches in my throat. Tony, the guy from the library. The guy who maybe fixes neighborhood cars. The guy who buys hot dogs for homeless people. What is he doing here?

He opens the closet door, slips his backpack off his shoulders, and crouches down. I watch him pull a small cardboard box, like one that would hold a coffee mug maybe, out of the bottom of the backpack and push it into the far corner of the closet. Then he zips the backpack, puts it back on his shoulders, and stands up.

I get right in his face. "What are you doing here?" I yell. "Tell me what was in that box." I try to push him, but my hand goes right through his shoulder. "Are you the one who kills me, Tony? Why are you here?"

I push him again, and this time I feel the smack of muscle on my fleshy palm. I'm not sure who it shocks more. Tony staggers back, panic all over his face as he frantically looks around the room. Seeing nothing, he walks very quickly back out into the living room.

I follow him. "That's right," I yell. "You should be scared of this place. You definitely shouldn't come back."

I step away from him long enough to go back to the wall and knock a few more times. This time every other knock gets through. When I turn back to Tony he's standing by the front door and he's really worried. His eyes are darting around every crevice, looking for the source of the noise. I get right in his face again and this time I focus all my energy on blowing air straight at him.

It doesn't work, at first, but I feel the difference the moment it does. The air slips past my lips for just a few seconds. Tony's hair blows off his forehead just a little, lifting in the stream of air I created. He shakes his head and reaches up to brush away a strand of hair with a shaking hand. "What the fuck?" he whispers.

"Get out of here," I whisper back. I feel the anger hot in my stomach. This guy, who I watched feed homeless people with a twenty-dollar bill he got from helping a neighbor out with his car. The same guy who I saw at the library and who local kids called "a good guy". This same guy is breaking into an empty unit in the middle of the night to leave a box. I wanted to trust this guy. I wanted to like this guy. I'm so angry that he may not be who I wanted him to be. "Run," I roar.

I feel the difference in my chest. The word vibrates between my breasts and up my throat. Tony staggers back from me, his eyes wide with true fear. He spots something over my shoulder, perhaps the back door, and makes a move toward it. He stumbles, one knee tagging the carpet for just a brief second before he's back on his feet. He tosses a glance over his shoulder, back where I'm standing and the momentum slams him into the wall separating the units. He grunts and grabs his left shoulder. Then he does exactly what he just heard me tell him to do. He runs. Straight out the back of the unit, across the lawn, and out of my sight.

It's me who pulls the back door shut. Then I sit down

on the kitchen floor to think. I just spoke a word out loud.

I spoke and Tony heard it.

I don't know what Tony was doing in this unit, I don't know if he'll come back or if I've scared him off. I only know that I just learned a new skill. I have to think about how to use this to my advantage.

chapter 26

I'm still sitting there trying to figure out what was different and how I talked when the cops arrive at the back door. The noises they make bring the memory back. Annie and Mom heard a noise. I turn my head and look behind me at the place where Tony slammed into the wall. That's what they heard. I suppose it's a good thing Tony was here, after all. Now the cops will look into this break-in. Maybe they can prevent it from happening again. Maybe I can use my new skill to communicate.

I stand up as if I'm going to greet the police officers, which is silly. They come in with their flashlights out. The beam cuts right through me, despite me waving my arms around like a fool trying to be seen. I rush to follow the first cop as he moves his way through the house.

He opens the bathroom door Tony closed earlier and looks around. That's when I remember the box. Tony left something behind. It will show them that he was here if I can get them to see it.

When he reaches the back bedroom, I slip through the closet door and sit on the floor next to the box, gesturing toward it. I try focusing on my frustration and anger. I try projecting. I just want him to see me because if he sees me, he'll see the box.

He shines his flashlight in the closet, uses it to look around, and then backs out of the space. My shoulders sag and I let out a sigh. The police officers are here because Annie and Mom heard a noise. Tiny cardboard boxes in empty closets don't make noise. Therefore, I suppose this box isn't exactly what he was looking for.

I make my way back out to the living room area, where he is now shining his light around and looking at the walls here. I see extra footprints on the hard floor, obvious markings that Tony was there. Of course this is the first time the police have been here, they won't notice a difference. In that moment I see it the way they will see it. There's no evidence of Tony being here.

Tony. That still shocks me. What was he doing here? Is it about hiding whatever is in that box? I make my way back to the closet, knowing there isn't much the police officers can or will do now. If I'm the only one who knows this box is here then it falls on me to find out what is in it.

The box is small, white, and unassuming. It has a little flap that holds the lid closed. I focus my energy on trying to pull that flap out. It takes me two tries, but it moves. Then I flip the top open on the first try.

I peek my head in, hoping to see something I recognize. Something obvious.

The first thing I see sitting on top of the box is a white rectangle that I recognize as an Arizona-issued ID card or driver's license. It's too dark to read all the text, but the picture looks like Tony. Why is he storing his ID card in a box in an empty unit?

I hear the door to the unit close, but decide what I'm doing is more interesting than whatever they're doing. Plus, I think I remember what they're doing. The police officer is about to give them a report and direct them to call the landlord. They will recommend the locks be changed. See, I already know this part. I don't, however, know what is in this box.

It takes me a few tries, but I manage to get the card out of the box. Actually, by the time it finally moves I'm pretty frustrated. So instead of lightly flicking it, I sort of fling it across the closet space. It lands upside down some distance away from me. I make a mental note to deal with it later.

Back in the cardboard box, I find a smaller box. Weird. This one is blue and white and small, about the size of a business card but thick. I concentrate and pull it slowly out of the box to bring it closer to my face. It's a box of contact lenses. Apparently, according to the label, they are tinted green. I drop them on the floor of the closet and lean back a little.

An ID card and a box of tinted contact lenses, that was your big hidden project? What is this guy up to?

I lean forward again, checking to see if the bottom of the small cardboard box is now visible. It's not. I stick my hand in and am greeted with something that is not exactly paper, because it's smoother and crinkles differently under my fingers. Cash. I close my fist and pull out the wad. Dropping it on the floor and smoothing it out, I count $280.

I decide I want a closer look at this ID I discarded now

that my eyes are a little more adjusted to the darkness. I lay my body out to stretch for the card. My foot slides awkwardly and I kick the box, which rattles. Rattling means it's not empty. I grab the ID card, pull it back toward me, and then sit up and turn my attention back to the box.

A purple rectangle sits at the bottom. I know that card, it's a Metro bus pass. Other than that pass, the box is empty. For real this time.

I squint at the ID. Definitely a picture of Tony, but possibly an older one because he has short hair in this one and the guy who just abandoned this strange box of items had long hair that almost reached his shoulders. It doesn't seem to matter how close I hold this card to my face, I cannot read that little black writing in the dark of the closet.

So I do the next best thing, I take the card and head outside with it. I pass right through the front wall into the driveway and stand under the light. Then I hold up my hand, but the card is gone. Confused, I look around me. Nothing.

I poke my head back through the wall and there is the card, sitting on the floor of the living room. Ok, so new thing I've learned. I can pass through solid objects. Other solid objects cannot. Right. Good lesson.

I fully pull myself back through the wall and into the unit. I cannot take the card through the wall so I do the next best thing. I pull back the front curtain to let in a little light. Now I can read the details of the card.

GRACE, CHRISTOPHER ALLEN

Wait, isn't his name Tony or Anthony? I try to remember how I knew that. Did he ever tell me? I don't think he did. I think the name was supplied by the people I met on the other street, the ones who knew him. Did anyone at the overpass call him by name? I'm frustrated that I can't remember. All these interactions and I can't even get his name right? Or, and this fact slowly drips into my brain like the trickle from a sink that leaks, this is a fake ID.

The address listed is incredibly familiar but, still, it takes me a second to process it. This is my address, sort of. The only difference is that this one says UNIT 1 whereas mine would say UNIT 2. Tony/Christopher is listing the empty unit as his address of record on what could be a fake ID.

I almost drop the card right then, my shock is so great. But something in my gut tells me to look at the eye color. Something tells me I'll already know the answer before I even look. I look anyway.

EYES GRN

I have a vivid memory, as Annie, of coming face-to-face with this guy at the library. Of being close enough to smell his cologne.

Tony's eyes are blue.

But those contact lenses he left in the box are green.

I'm not a total idiot. This is a kit someone would need if they were changing into someone else. The only question is, why does he have it and why is it in this unit?

And, perhaps more importantly, what does it have to do with me and my death?

chapter 27

Those revelations feel big. Big enough to keep me from realizing that I just seamlessly interacted with a lot of physical things in a row without having to pause and focus. As if remembering its limitations, my hand drops the ID card onto the floor. I think back. I wasn't focused from the moment I picked up that ID card. The money was easy. I felt it right away, I pulled it out right away. I even kicked the box when I was only focused on the ID card.

Is it possible I'm getting better at this?

I reach for the curtain, ready to pull it all the way open and flood the room with the light from the street lamp. My hand goes right through it.

It's almost like I'm trying too hard. Like something in my body knows how to do this and I'm capable of being good at it when I'm incredibly angry or completely distracted. With a little practice, maybe I could —

I stop myself. I don't need to practice being a good ghost or whatever I am. I need to figure out why Tony is hiding this stuff in this unit and stop him from whatever happens that ends up with me being dead. I won't need to be a good ghost if I'm still alive.

So what do I know about Tony? Let's review.

1.   He must live near here because I've never seen him drive a car.

2.   I've seen him at two different houses on the next street over. One time he was getting cash for fixing a car. That means he likely does work of some kind around here, too.

3.   I know he shops at that convenience store on the corner.

4.   He visits the overpass, sometimes bringing food. They knew him there.

5.   He sometimes goes to the library.

I walk through the wall at the back of the house and head to the street that has helped me find Tony twice now. I sit cross-legged on the ground literally in the middle of the road and wait. I don't have to get up for anything, Tony. I'm not missing you this time.

As it was at the basketball court, time must pass even though I can't feel anything different. The sun eventually rises, meaning I'm officially on Day 4 since moving into the house (I think) and drawing closer to my eventual demise. I try not to think about that. I tell myself I'm doing the best thing I can right now by looking for Tony. He's my new favorite suspect, whether he likes it or not.

The neighborhood starts coming to life around me, slowly stretching its limbs. Cars start and people back out of driveways. I let them drive right through me because I'm not leaving until I see Tony. People come out in sneakers and shorts, some carrying leashes with dogs eager to run, some with headphones firmly in place ready to run themselves. I even spot Ali, the neighborhood girl who could turn out to be a great friend if I can get this right. She has a digital camera around her neck and she's walking away from the main road. For a brief second, I long to follow her. I want to see what in this neighborhood is worth taking the time to view through a lens. But I have more important things to do. Besides, if I can stop my death there will be plenty of time for photography in my future.

The door of a house nearby slams and someone's angry footsteps start stomping down the sidewalk. I recognize the hair just a split second before the face. There he is. I jump up and dash across the street, literally getting in his face and almost wishing he knew I was here. "Where are we going, Tony? What's the plan today?"

Naturally, he ignores me. He keeps up his angry walk in the direction of the convenience store. I stay right next to him, keeping pace with him all the way. He doesn't go into the little store but follows the path directly to the overpass. "Tony," someone calls as soon as he's nearby.

I feel vindicated with the confirmation of his real name. Christopher is, in fact, a cover. What is this guy hiding?

He saunters up to the guy who called him, his footsteps quieter as if he is feeling calmer now. They exchange a fist bump. "You need anything today?" Tony asks.

"I need to know what's going on with you. That's what I need," the guy answers. I recognize him as the same guy who asked Tony where he was living the last time we were all under this overpass together.

"I'm working on something, don't worry about me. You need something to drink or eat, maybe? We could go grab something. My treat," Tony says.

The guy shakes his head. "Tell me more about this thing you're working on. Are you getting yourself out of that house?"

"Yeah, I think so. It's in the works." Tony leans a little closer and drops his voice. "I may have something that will work for you and me, but you'd have to be willing to accept a few changes."

The guy nods slowly. "Are we talking about leaving town?"

Tony pulls back and shoves his hands in his pockets. "You know I can't do that yet. I have things to take care of first. We'll have to start with names. If I don't do that he'll find me. I have to be drastic."

"Leaving town would be drastic, anything else is just stupid."

This guy clearly knows more about Tony's situation than I do. I step so close that I'm practically between them as if I can learn some of the secrets they are sharing just by proximity. Who is this third dangerous guy they're talking about? Could I have been wrong about Tony? Could the real threat be the guy he's running from?

"It's not stupid. It's perfect. He'd never expect it. He doesn't look for you here, does he? He never thinks about what could be right under his nose."

The older man shakes his head so hard that long hairs fly right through me and make me flinch. "He doesn't look for me like he'd look for you. My brother cares more about his son than he ever could about me and you know that. It's about control. He has more control over you than he does over me right now. We can agree that you have to get the hell out of there, but you have to be safe about it."

Tony smiles and takes a little step back. He looks carefree, suddenly. As if he's slipped on a costume of someone with a normal life. "I'm being safe, I promise. Give me forty-eight hours to tie up loose ends and I'll be back for you. This will work out." He turns around, pointing his feet back the way he came. "Are you joining me for breakfast or not?"

The older man shakes his head. "Not today, kid. Be careful out there, all right?"

"Always," Tony answers.

I follow him out of the overpass area and along the main road away from my house. I'm more confused than I was before this visit. I walk beside him, talking mostly to myself about what is happening. "You are trying to run away from someone dangerous, I get that. Your father? That guy called him your father. But he also called the guy his brother. So that's your uncle over there. I guess that explains why you are so generous with the food. You want a way for your uncle and you to safely get away from your father, that's what I'm getting. What makes you think you can just take over the unit next door? Is that what happens? Do you kill me because I try to stop you or something? I don't plan on stopping you, but maybe there are things I don't know." I shake my head. Obviously, there are plenty of things I don't know. "Maybe it's not you that's dangerous. Maybe your father finds you living in that unit and kills me? Why me though? That's a different problem."

We're now two streets away from the convenience store and I'm no closer to figuring any of this out. I jump in front of him. "Who is the dangerous one, Tony?" I shout.

He stops and spins around, eyes searching. A man with headphones walks past us, Tony reaches out and taps him on the arm. "Did you just call me?" he asks.

The guy takes a headphone out. "What?"

"Did you say my name?" Tony's eyes are wide, his energy suddenly frantic.

I try to touch him, my hand goes right through. "You heard me?" I ask. "You heard me say your name and you think it was this poor guy."

"I don't even know your name, kid." The guy shakes his arm free, puts his headphone back in, and jogs off shaking his head.

Tony runs a hand down his face and takes off. "Wait, where are we going?" I shout. Of course, whatever I did to get him to hear me a second ago has passed. Tony keeps walking. I jog to catch back up, falling in step beside him.

Four streets down from mine, he turns. I notice he's walking faster now as if getting closer to wherever he was going has given him energy. He walks right up the driveway of a little blue house and knocks on a white front door. A girl opens the door just a little, peeking to see who is there.

"Oh, hey Tony. I forgot you were coming by today. Hang on." She disappears again. Tony shoves his hands in his pockets and rocks on his feet, waiting.

Finally, she reappears at the door, holding a backpack out toward him. "This is everything," she says. Tony takes the bag and unzips it. He looks inside, moving contents around. I get in between his face and the bag, also looking. I see some fabric at the bottom of the bag, possibly a blanket. Then there's a lighter and a knife.

The flash of memory is back. Sharp pain in my gut and the vision of blood dripping through my fingers.

I pull back when the memory stops and look at Tony's face. Nothing. No reaction at all.

But me? I'm feeling a reaction. A strong, visceral, animal reaction. It's like anger but hotter and more raw. That knife is tied to my painful memories of my death, I'm suddenly sure of it.

It's not his Dad that I have to worry about. Tony is going to kill me. I have to warn Annie.

chapter 28

How best to get a message to Annie? Options:

1. Write a note somewhere. It would have to be somewhere she would see it, but somewhere Mom wouldn't because Mom wouldn't understand. Also, how the heck can I reliably hold a pen for long enough to write a note? This isn't the best plan.

2. Focus on making myself real enough to shout to her, like I shouted to Tony. Of course, I shouted exactly one word to Tony and I'd need more than that for Annie. If I try to shout too many words at her she may panic, like Tony did, and run off. I need to talk to her but I need her to stay put long enough to hear the message.

Cue another big lightbulb moment where my comic book self would shout "Eureka". Where better to get a teenager to spend time listening to something other than a phone? This may be my best idea yet. I will use a phone somewhere, channel all my energy, call Annie, and talk to her. She can listen without noticing I happen to be without a body at the moment and am, therefore, threatening. Plus, if I talk a little differently maybe she won't notice it's essentially her own voice.

I like this plan.

Now I just have to find a way to make a phone call. I take my time moving slowly through the neighborhood, watching everyone who passes. I see a few people with cell phones in their hands, obviously, but that doesn't seem very helpful. How would I get the phone out of their hand, unlocked, and use it to make a call? Plus there's the problem of holding the phone. I would need them to hold it for me, which isn't going to happen.

I end up back near the overpass. I don't even fully realize where I am right away. Someone coughs and it draws my attention to the group of homeless people living there. Today they're huddled in the shade. I spot open water bottles in most of their hands. I cannot feel the heat right now beating down on my shoulders and neck but I remember what it felt like. It just makes me feel worse.

I make my way over to the man Tony has been coming to meet. "You're his uncle, aren't you?" I ask. I know he can't hear me. I'm desperate. I have to keep trying these things, hoping that one of them will result in something that works. "Tell him to stay away from the empty house. Tell him he's going to do something wrong if he keeps going there."

He stands up and shoves his hands in his pocket. "Anyone got a hot tip on a panhandling location for me?" he asks. "I could use a cup of coffee."

"Just go to the store. They'll be swapping coffee at the top of the hour. Sometimes they'll let you take a cup before they pour it out."

"Maybe I'll do that," he says. "I could always use the

extra cash for the kid though. If anyone gets anything remember to put it in the Tony fund."

"Yeah, right after I pay off my Mercedes," someone calls. There are a few laughs.

"He's always done right by us," the uncle continues. "Don't be a jackass."

I wander away from the conversation, which is making me uncomfortable. It's not that I don't like Tony. I actually do, which is part of the problem here. I want him to be a good person. I want him to not be the guy responsible for all of this.

I have to keep Annie out of that house. I have to find a way to call her.

I head to the convenience store because I can't think of where else I can find a phone. There's a pay phone, but I have no pockets full of change on this particular ghostly outfit. So, I try inside.

There's a phone under the counter. I stand beside the counter, it's not like I'm bothering someone, and wait while the clerk helps customers. I figure all I need is a few minutes when the store is empty so no one questions me using the phone. I can wait. We've already established that I wait better than most humans.

Finally, there's a lull in customers. The store is empty. The clerk walks off toward the coffee area. I figure it'll take a few minutes to make a few pots of coffee. This is my chance.

I close my eyes and focus, knocking the phone off the hook on the second try. Then I punch the numbers for Annie's cell phone. I lean down close to the receiver, waiting. A weird beeping starts in my ear. Not like a message pending, but like an error. Frustrated, I push the little hang-up button.

What am I doing wrong?

There's a cellphone on the counter. Face up and screen lit. He must have just been using it. This is a stupid idea, but it's the best idea I have. If I wait too long, it'll go to sleep, and then I'll probably need a passcode that I don't have to unlock the device. I can't hesitate. I touch the phone button on the bottom of the screen and the call pad comes up.

I check on the clerk. He's emptied and rinsed two pots and is currently reaching for a third. I haven't heard a coffee grinder fire up yet, so I'm hoping I still have time while he makes a new pot.

I dial Annie's number.

The phone rings. I leave it sitting there on the counter and lean close to it. I figure I won't have a lot of time because the clerk will hear me too. I have to focus on sounding real but not overly loud. I can do this.

I take deep breaths while I wait out her/our message telling me to leave a message.

Then, I try my hardest to be a physical thing.

"Annie, you have to stay away from Tony. You remember Tony, right? He's the guy you saw when you met those kids on the next street over. He's blond with blue eyes. You saw him at the library later. Anyway, he's DANGEROUS." I feel like that word was louder. I wonder how much of this is getting through, but I don't have time to try again. I just have to keep going.

I check on the clerk. He's grinding beans now, it's loud enough to cover me. I let my volume increase. "This part is important. LISTEN. You have to STAY OUT OF THE HOUSE NEXT DOOR. It's dangerous. I don't care what you hear or what you see. STAY OUT. Just trust me, please." The grinder stops. I glance at the screen. The numbers are just past 2 minutes and 10 seconds. I hope that's enough. "I have to go. Stay home."

I push the red button on the phone just as the counter ticks to 2 minutes, 17 seconds and the clerk starts walking back in my direction. I duck below the counter, on instinct. I notice I left the receiver off the hook on the phone down here. I try to focus on it. I manage to get the receiver to move, but I drop it before it's on the cradle. The clerk comes behind the counter and frowns at it. "Stupid phone," he mumbles. He picks it up and puts it to his ear. Then he shrugs and drops it back on the cradle for me.

That's when the memory comes back. The memory of Annie listening to a message on her phone, using her thumb to fast-forward through the entire 2 minutes and 17 seconds. Blank. The entire message was blank.

I drop down on the floor and wrap my arms around my knees, the picture of absolute frustration. I have no idea how else to get a message to Annie. That was my best idea and I have a feeling I just recorded dead air on my cell phone, which is not at all helpful.

I'm running out of time and I am no closer to preventing this tragedy.

chapter 29

I have never felt more useless than I do that afternoon. I was given this one extra chance. One chance to change everything that I know is coming. Instead of making a difference, I appear to be floundering around town, causing noise and chaos in the empty unit next door, and possibly just falling into the pattern of repeating whatever causes me to die. I've been trying not to focus on that, but I don't see how I can ignore this latest proof. When I was Annie, because I clearly WAS Annie and have all her memories even if they are patchy, I received that phone call while I was waiting on the locksmith to finish up. I listened to that 2-minute and 17-second dead air message while I was standing there, tapping my foot and being a typical teenager. So how is it possible that I both MADE that blank phone message and LISTENED to that phone message at two different times?

Seriously, if I had a head that functioned like a typical head right now, it would be throbbing. I cannot handle this. It's entirely unfair. This is a rigged game in an unfair system and I'm about to lose. Really, I'm about to lose twice. I have the crushing loss of my life to look forward to as Annie and the epic failure that is letting myself die because I can't solve this puzzle to look forward to in this current ghostly form.

I stop my little angry tirade, which was currently taking the form of stomping around the empty parking lot of the convenience store, and look in the direction of the duplex again. I cannot give up. I realize that's what I was just on the verge of doing and I can't let myself do that. I was given a redo. I have one chance. If I just stay here in this parking lot going all Casper on the employees and shoppers I will not save Annie. I have to try something, even if it fails.

I head back to the empty unit and resume my pacing in front of the wall between the kitchens instead. I need another plan and in the absence of a plan pacing is the only thing I seem to be able to do. I've already decided getting a message to Annie needs to be priority number one. She has to stay out of this unit and away from Tony. All I need is for her to make it a few hours longer than I did. Then I succeed. Heck, I can assume if she makes it two seconds longer than I did I'll take over her body again and we get to keep going. I just have to keep her out of this unit where Tony appears to be trying to set up shop.

Frustrated with the lack of ideas coming to me in this unit, I float through the wall and into Annie's kitchen. Everything is quiet over here. Thanks to the back window Mom loves so much I also notice it's nighttime. Somehow I've lost an entire afternoon that should've been full of great plans and action to pouting about my situation and stomping my way around town. I have to come up with something, I'm running out of time.

The problem is that I am still completely without a

good plan. So, I resume my pacing, this time in Annie's kitchen. There's a cabinet door slightly ajar above the counter. Do I get to stay a ghost-type entity if I don't succeed, I wonder? Could it be worth it to try and practice ghostly skills?

I push the cabinet closed on my second try.

Then I pull it back open on my first.

Inside the cabinet are a few spices that Mom buys in larger containers that don't fit on her spice rack. There are also large bags of sugar and flour. Flour, something about that is calling to me, for some reason. Again, it's that weird sensation like I should have a memory of this but it's not quite there. Like maybe it was a dream I can't remember now that I'm awake. Of course, in reality, it's probably something related to Annie or maybe something that hasn't happened yet.

I reach out for the bag, intending to grab it.

I stop myself. My hand is literally frozen halfway to the bag of flour. Maybe this is the answer. Maybe I ignore my instinct to do whatever comes with that random tickling of my memory. I can't play into this stuff. I'm pacing around here angry that I feel like I tricked myself by just replaying the past. I forced Annie to listen to that message, just like I listened to that message. Whatever Annie is going to do with flour, I shouldn't be a part of it. I need to avoid the flour. Then the flour thing never happens to Annie and I changed the timeline. Once the timeline is changed, it can't be changed back. Right? Maybe that will keep Annie from whatever makes her dead.

Yes, that's what I'll do. I'll ignore this stupid flour and find something else to focus on. I slam the cabinet on the first try. The noise is incredibly satisfying, echoing through the house. But it makes me pause, listening to the sounds that might mean I woke up Mom and Annie. When there's nothing, I pull the cabinet open and slam it again just to enjoy the satisfying slam in replay.

Except that this time the slam shakes the bag loose and flour topples out of the cabinet, opening and spilling everywhere on its way down.

"You have got to be kidding me," I yell. "I was trying to keep you in the cabinet." I push the bag. "You stupid, ridiculous, can't-stay-where-you-belong-in-the-cabinet bag." I close my eyes and tip my head back toward the ceiling. Ok, I have to calm down. The flour is now all over the countertop and a little on the floor. I can't remember why flour seemed important, but I can't change it now. It's already in play.

Maybe I can make use of it.

I focus all my energy, which I have been so good at doing lately, on the flour. I try to make a little mark in it with my finger. It works. The flour scoots out of the path of my finger and leaves the black counter showing through.

Maybe I can leave Annie a message in the flour. Something simple. Something obvious that will just warn her away. I wanted to warn Annie, I wanted to leave Mom out of it. After all, I want to avoid whatever causes my death, not just cause a different one. But desperate times call for chaos or something. Plus, the flour is already here. I can't do anything about that now.

I'm going to leave a message. I just have to figure out the easiest and best way to get this all across. I want something short so "STAY OUT OF THE EMPTY UNIT UNLESS

YOU WANT TO DIE A GRUESOME DEATH" is probably too much. The counter is covered in flour but it's not a huge counter. Plus, the longer the message the more I have to focus and write. I need something shorter. "STAY OUT OF THE EMPTY UNIT" while great is probably also too long. "STAY OUT" doesn't make sense. It's not clear enough. "EMPTY UNIT" is better but doesn't give enough information. Still, maybe if I get her thinking about the empty unit they'll go look at it. Maybe they'll find the box full of Tony's identity change stuff and call the police. But "EMPTY UNIT" is still a bit long. Maybe just shorten it?

E U

I almost don't even realize my fingertip has traced the letters onto the counter at first. It's like I was in some kind of trance. Why my finger interacted with the flour when I wasn't focused is a mystery that I am not capable of solving right now. I'm not even capable of thinking about it right this second. The bottom line is I just wrote EU in the flour on the counter.

How is that at all helpful?

I stare at it, wondering how I can fix this. Annie won't know what the heck EU is supposed to be. This is awful. How can I save this?

I think I hear a noise coming from the back of the house. Is Mom awake already? I need more time. I have to figure out how to save this.

Quickly, and with concentration going in and out like a whiteboard marker that's running out of ink, I run my finger underneath the initials and leave what I hope is a clearer word.

DANGER

It will have to be enough.

Chapter 30

Operation "give Annie a message" has been put into motion. I refuse to hang around in this place longer and watch if she gets the message. I've tried with the books, the phone, and now this. I need another plan now. Priority 1 was the message. Priority 2 needs to be Tony. He's still my best suspect, especially now that I know he has the knife that gives me that memory. This is it, if the sun is up we're on Day 5. I'm just about out of time.

I leave the house by floating my way through the front door and stand there on the stoop, thinking. Where can I find Tony today?

These memory snippets are strange. Just standing here trying to remember, I get this flash of memory like a photograph. A quick flash of being in a park and seeing Tony with someone. Ali is there, with her camera. Is that today? Does that happen today?

I'm finding that park.

I may not have a fully formed memory, but it appears my feet do. I manage to find the park on the first try and park myself near a tree that I also feel drawn to. I'm not there for a long time, I don't think, before Ali shows up with a bag and starts assembling her camera.

I haven't spent a lot of time in this form hanging around Ali. This is a good chance to learn about her, I suppose. Right away I notice she has a camera of similar quality to mine. A name brand common for photographers, but nothing overly fancy. Just your average high-end digital camera. She does have a few impressive lenses tucked into that camera bag, but the one she pulls out is a pretty wide lens. Something tugs at my memory, something about landscape shots.

I settle in to watch Ali for a while, taking note of her decent form and the photo she appears to be framing. She's got talent and patience, two things my photography teacher was always trying to instill in us. I watch her for long enough that I'm starting to wonder why I'm here. Then I show up. I mean, Annie shows up.

The interaction between the two of us is strange to watch. I see Annie take in everything I just noticed again, the camera and the skill Ali works with. Then I watch myself settle in to try and get a decent shot of the bird's nest that Ali pointed out.

Again, my mind wanders, wondering if this is a good waste of my limited time sitting here watching the afternoon play out in the same way it did before. Then Tony walks into the park. I notice him first because Annie and Ali are behind their lenses.

He stands on the grass just inside what would be considered part of the park and looks around. That backpack I've seen him with many times before is hooked over his shoulders. I wonder if the knife is still in there or if he's dropped it off.

I get closer to him, feeling my anger rising with each step I take in his direction. Then Tony spots someone and immediately starts walking. He walks with a purpose as if he needs to get something done and has more important places to be. I can empathize with the feeling. Tony doesn't slow down until he's crossed the park to within five feet of a taller guy.

The memory comes back. Ali says this new guy is "bad news" and warns Annie to stay away from him. Could this be the guy? Maybe Tony is innocent. Maybe he's about to hand over that knife.

I run to catch up with them. Tony speaks first, his voice low and somehow dangerous. "You got it?"

"You could get one of these anywhere, you know. We didn't need to do this whole cloak and dagger routine." He shakes his head while simultaneously reaching into the back pocket of his jeans and pulling out what appears to be an old-school cell phone. "One throw-away cell phone, prepaid with the amount you gave me minus my finders fee. You'll need another one in about a month unless you make a lot of phone calls."

Tony takes the phone, flips it open, pushes a button, and snaps it closed again when the button registers with a chime noise. "Thanks," he says. "We're square?"

"We're square."

"No one saw you buy it?"

Again, the tall guy shakes his head. "Who the fuck would care that I bought a throwaway, Tony? Use your head."

"Right." He shoves the phone way down deep into his

front pocket. "I'll get in touch if I need another one," he says. "Thanks."

"Whatever, man." The guy points behind Tony. "Get out of here before my next deal walks up."

When Tony backs up, I follow him. I get right in his face. "Ok," I say as if he can hear me. "So we have a disposable cell phone now to go with the rest of your disappearing kit. What's the problem? Do you think I saw you?" I stop and think. I did see him. Annie and Ali saw him having a conversation with this guy. But we didn't know what he bought. We didn't know he bought anything. The memory is hazy, but I think I thought it was drugs. "We didn't see anything important. That can't be it or you'd also be targeting Ali. Why me, Tony? What happens?"

Tony continues to ignore me, traveling back toward the neighborhood. I follow him even when we end up on the next street over. I follow him through the door of a house I think I've seen Tony coming out of before.

We're not alone. There's a man in a white shirt sitting on a recliner in front of the television. He has a beer in his right hand and the remote control for the TV in his left. He uses the latter to mute the show. "Where have you been?" he barks, his voice hoarse and raspy.

"Out," Tony says. "I'm not staying long." He continues to the other side of the room, toward a hallway.

"You owe me rent."

Tony stops in the hallway, keeping his back to the man. "I just gave you rent a week ago. Most people only pay once a month."

"Most people aren't useless assholes without a job."

Tony takes a deep breath and I can see him clench his jaw as if he might be grinding his teeth. "I'll get you more tomorrow." He resumes walking and, again, I follow.

"Is this the Dad you talked about? I get it, he's kind of a jerk. Is this why you're leaving? Maybe your Uncle is right. Maybe you aren't going far enough away. Maybe you should go further." I stop in the hallway because it somehow feels wrong to follow him into the bedroom.

"I have to go back," I tell him, continuing the conversation I wish we were having. "I have to keep Annie away from you. It would really help me a lot if you just didn't show up at that empty unit again, ok? Please."

When he doesn't answer and the TV in the other room starts blaring again, I head back to the duplex. I have no idea what else to do.

chapter 31

I have no better plan than this: pacing back and forth in the backyard of the house, waiting for something to happen. If the idea is to witness the crime, I'm in the perfect spot. If the point is to stop it from happening, I'm useless! What am I supposed to do when Tony shows up? I can't stop him, not physically. I can try to scare him off again, maybe that will work. I can try to alert Annie, although that may not be the best idea. I can't call the police, but I suppose if things get desperate I can always … what? Throw things, I guess. Yes, that will be me, throwing random things from around the yard at a guy I thought was cool as he comes to kill the other version of me.

Oh my God, this is so unfair.

No matter how angry I get, I can't come up with a better plan. So guess what I'm currently doing? Pacing the yard, waiting for something to happen, and practicing kicking rocks so later I can use that skill to throw things and try to scare Tony.

It's a terrible plan that seems destined to fail, but it's literally the only thing I have.

I decide to check in on the other me just to make sure

she's still safe. I float my way into the unit occupied by Mom and Annie and pause in the kitchen, taking the time to analyze every detail like some tiny piece I may have missed could be the answer to the most important test question later. Annie is happily stirring food and humming to herself as if she doesn't have a care in the world. I notice with a pang that she's wearing the same outfit as me. This combines with her careless humming to make me irrationally sad so I make the rest of the sweep of the house quick and pop right back outside. Mom appears to not be home yet.

Outside, the back door of the empty unit looks solid and the lock is shiny and new. This tells me the locksmith arrived as I remember. The unit itself is still empty except for the cardboard box and random contents Tony left behind. Everything appears to be exactly where it was last dropped, nothing has been moved. That means Tony hasn't been back again.

A car door at the front surprises me until I remember that it's likely just Mom. I float my way through the wall connecting the units just to confirm and find her and Annie having a quick conversation in the kitchen. They both look exhausted. I remember exhaustion, sort of. I remember it the way you remember your kindergarten class. It's like a hazy memory of an experience, nothing sharp or clear.

I stand there and debate my options. I can sit here and let the evening play out around me, enjoying the memories that would become my final night on earth if I mess this up. I can resume pacing around out back, waiting for something to happen. Or, I can attempt to find Tony.

Attempting to find Tony has big risks. Namely that I won't find him and he'll appear here at the house while I'm running around in some other part of town looking for him. We know how it ends if Tony is here and I have done nothing to stop it. I have no choice but to throw that plan out.

That means my options are back to sit here and wallow in my own memories by painfully watching Annie and Mom have a normal evening or pace the backyard and give myself the sense that I'm doing something productive.

It's no wonder that I end up back outside.

The sun drops below the horizon, which I have to admit looks kind of cool. It makes my fingers itch for the weight of my camera and the pressure of the shutter button. I purposely turn my back on the beauty of nature and force myself to keep up the pacing. My legs don't get tired, no matter how many laps I do around the yard. That means I don't have to flop myself down on the floor or risk falling asleep, two things that would've plagued the previous version of Annie if she were the one out here keeping watch.

The world is really quiet after dark. I don't think I've ever noticed that before. The hum of the traffic starts to fall away and the sound of laughter and life drops off until there's just this sense of quiet and calm. Like the whole world is holding its breath in anticipation.

That's how quiet it gets around here. I stand there, in the backyard, enjoying the quiet. Underneath the calm I'm sort of feeling, I still feel that sense of stress. I have to get this right. But it's almost like all of that is happening to someone else. It can't be happening to me today, because today feels completely calm. The world feels satisfied right now.

Someone inside the house drops something and the noise shatters the calm like broken cell phone glass. I almost laugh at myself for jumping. I turn my body and look at the back windows. Our window is dark. Annie and Mom have gone to bed. How long ago was that? When did the light go out? I don't remember them going to bed. I can't remember them even finishing dinner. How much time have I lost?

I move closer to the window, squinting inside and looking for Annie. I'm sure she's got to be awake, moving around in there. She has to be the one who dropped something.

A flashlight beam cuts through the window of the empty unit, casting light onto the ground in the backyard. Panic fills me. Suddenly I feel the dread of knowing it's too late. It's heavy in my stomach as if I swallowed lead. I feel like I'm going to throw up. This is the exact opposite of calm. This is it. The moment where I find a miracle and save my own life, or the biggest failure I'll ever experience.

I move through the wall slowly, dreading what I will find. The kitchen of this unit looks the same as it did when I last checked it. I spin myself around and look at the back door. The lock is shiny and new, freshly changed by the locksmith. How did Tony get himself in here? I assume it's Tony. I've been assuming it's Tony all this time.

What if it's not?

I move through the house, forgetting for an instant that no one can see me and I don't need to be quiet. I pick up speed. Someone is crouched on the ground in front of the box.

I recognize the backpack he's wearing, it's the same one I watched the girl from the neighborhood hand him. The same one that had the knife inside. If I could cry in this form, tears would be flowing.

He's holding the cash in his hand, moving through the bills at a steady pace. Having counted it he shoves it back into the box. Then he looks up, shining a flashlight around the room. It's strange to see the emotions on his face. If I knew him better I might be able to figure out what they are. Instead, I just see what looks like fear. Then he puts everything else back in the cardboard box and stands up.

I get closer, right in his face. I can't think of what else to do. I fall back to what I would've done in my old body. "Tony, how did you get in here?" I shout.

Tony walks right through me. He picks up a sleeping bag and unrolls it in the room like he's claiming this area for his own. He looks like a kid who is just getting ready for a camping trip or a sleepover. He doesn't look dangerous. He doesn't look scary.

Then my eyes fall on the rest of the things he's brought with him today. Right on top of the open backpack is the knife. It has a long black handle, thick and textured. The blade shines in the beam of the flashlight. It's at least ten inches long. One side is smooth but the other is jagged. It's the scariest thing I have ever seen in my life. Seeing it here, in the place where Annie will die if I get this wrong, it's utterly debilitating.

I stare at it, unable to take my eyes away. The shadows move around me, the flashlight beam causes the knife to light up in different parts, almost making it feel like it is moving. But still, I can't look away.

A memory flashes behind my eyes. A memory that I can't fully see. A memory of blood and pain.

That moves me. This knife causes that pain, I'm sure of it.

Think, Annie, think.

Alright, Tony is here. He is moving around the room setting up some kind of camping situation. Clearly, he intends to stay here. Maybe he's making too much noise? I glance at the wall. Yes, that's it. Annie hears him and comes over to investigate. Maybe she scares him?

I should get him out of here.

I get closer, really get in his face. I focus all my energy on my hand and push on his shoulder. Nothing happens. I extend a finger and think about how angry he is getting me. He shouldn't be here. He shouldn't be threatening Annie. I poke him in the shoulder.

I feel the difference. The shoulder pushes back, soft and unsuspecting. Tony looks at it and an emotion I do recognize is clear on his face, panic. I have felt that panic, shades of it anyway. "Who's there?" he whispers. "Go away."

I don't go away. Instead, I do it harder. Again my finger meets that resistance. This time the poke jerks his shoulder back further. He swats at me but his hand passes right through. "Stop," he says. "This has to happen. Stop."

What the heck does that mean? He's getting louder. I can't have him getting louder. I lean closer to him. "Run," I yell. It doesn't come out as a yell. It comes out as a whisper. But it comes out.

"Fuck you," he yells. Then he grabs the knife by the handle and drops himself onto the sleeping bag. "I'm staying right here." He holds the knife up in front of him.

This is bad.

I turn in a circle, my brain whirling. "I'm trying to get you to leave. I have to scare you off. You can't be here. You can't be here." My voice cracks so that when I say it a third time, it sounds like a plea. "You can't be here." I drop onto my knees in front of him, really begging now. "Tony, please, get out of here."

He doesn't move. His eyes dart around the room, checking every corner. I've made it worse, I realize. I've set him off. I've put him right on the edge where he's the most dangerous. I have to fix this.

I jump to my feet. New plan. If I can't get Tony to leave, I have to get Annie to ignore him. I have to give Annie something else to focus on. Yes, that will work. That has to work.

I head outside of the unit and around the back. I cross all the way to the far wall. The wall that puts me as far away from Tony and his scary knife as possible without leaving the plot of land. I use all my energy to tap on the wall. I keep it up, consistently tapping. C'mon, Annie. Get up, come out here. Move away from the unit.

Eventually, I see her. She comes around the back of the house, heading straight for me. She looks confused, then relieved. I remember, in a flash, how she didn't know what was going on when she came out here. She wasn't sure what she would find. My eyes follow hers up to the tree branches. I remember that's what she thought made the noise.

Fine, I have her out here. Now, the next step is to figure out how to get her to notice something is wrong and call the police for us. I can do that. Keep her out of the house and get her to call the police. Does she have her phone? I can't remember if I grabbed it. It doesn't matter. If I can get her near that front window she will see the flashlight beam. Then she'll know something is up and she'll call. I know she will. I know how Annie thinks. Flashlight equals panic equals cops.

New plan. Get Annie to the front of the house. Get her to see the flashlight in the front window. Call the cops.

I move closer to her and lean in. "Come this way, please." I know my voice doesn't ring out in the quiet. I feel the absence of it from my vocal cords. But she looks in my direction anyway, almost as if she heard me.

"Follow me," I say. I head to the front of the house.

Annie follows me, but slowly. "That's right, just this way," I tell her. But I move quickly, I move ahead of her to the middle of the yard. Yes, from here you can tell there is a light back there. The black curtains that have blocked that window for as long as she's lived here have a sort of gray hue in the center. I know she'll freak out when she sees that.

A renewed sense of urgency moves me back to Annie. "I know this is weird," I tell her. "But we're almost there. I just need to show you one thing. Please. Go to the window. Look at the window."

Annie's feet move her in that direction. Seriously, though, she's moving really slowly.

I have time. I'm going to just make sure Tony is still in

there. I can't have him turning off that flashlight the second before she sees it or something.

I fly through the wall and stand in front of Tony. He's still in the same position, sitting cross-legged on the sleeping bag. He's holding the knife out in front of him and I can tell he's scared. Sweat is beading on his forehead.

In the quiet of this unit, you can hear Annie's footsteps in the front yard. Tony hears it too because he jumps to his feet. The knife is still in front of him, but now his arm looks more ready for something. It's cocked at the elbow. This is so bad, he's making me really nervous. I don't know how to calm him down. Plus, I have to get back to Annie. Annie has to call the cops. That has to happen.

Back out front, check on Annie. "Flashlight in the window. That's what I need you to see. See it, call the cops. Please, Annie."

Annie's eyes were on her front door but they flick in my direction. They fall on the unit next door. "Yes, this unit. See the light? Call the cops." I jump up and down. "Annie, come on. See it."

She looks like she is looking in the right direction. I can't have her miss it. I duck back into the unit. Maybe I'll grab the flashlight and move it. That will make the light jump. She won't miss that. I see the flashlight, sitting in the middle of the floor pointing up toward the ceiling. But I also see Tony. He's moved toward the front door now. He's directly next to it, arm pulled back.

I'm almost to the flashlight when I hear Annie's footsteps hit the concrete out front. Tony tenses. My eyes fall on the doorknob.

The doorknob that looks exactly like the one in our unit. The doorknob with the small raised locking mechanism, the one that is so easy to turn from this side of the unit. The one that is clearly turned perpendicular to the floor.

No, no. The third time I try to scream the word it actually comes out of my mouth. "No," the sound echoes through the entire unit.

The front door is unlocked.

The handle spins. The fourth time I scream, it is in echo with Annie's scream as the front door opens. Tony's reaction is instant. There's no chance of me getting there before it happens. I watch the knife sink into Annie's stomach until the only visible part is the handle.

Then, everything goes black.

IN BETWEEN

chapter 32

"No, damn it." I stomp my feet in the empty gray room.

I never wanted to be back in this empty gray room again. But, suddenly, it gives me hope. What if there's a second, or more precisely, a third chance? I turn in circles, looking for her.

She pops in on my third circle. "Hello, Annie. How did it go?" It's the same woman I remember from the last time I was here. This time her dark hair is pulled back in a bun close to her head, but she's wearing the same flowy dress and ratty sneakers.

"That doesn't count," I yell. I move closer to her, but I

don't lower my voice. "I didn't know the front door was open. How long was the front door open? This time I'll do it right."

"How did you think Anthony gained entrance to the unit?" she asks, tilting her head to the right like a dog hearing a strange noise.

I open and close my mouth a few times, trying to think of something. The back door and the crisp new lock were my clues. My shoulders sag. "I missed it." I shake off the disappointment and step closer to her. This time, my voice is in a normal range. "Let me try again. I'll just lock that door early before he can even get in. Then everything will be better."

She sighs. "Annie, dear, most people don't even get the chance you got."

I feel tears pricking my eyes. "But, my Mom …" I let my voice trail off.

She steps closer and puts her arm around my shoulders. She's so solid and warm. I want to sink into the human contact she's offering. It feels like I've been without it for so long and something about this woman just feels so safe. I feel the tears slip down my cheeks. "Let's have a seat. I need to tell you a few really important things." She gestures with her left hand and I notice two comfy-looking armchairs have appeared in the room. Of course, they're also gray.

I nod and we cross the room and drop into the chairs. They are more comfortable than I even imagined. I think I missed sitting down.

She sits up, her shoulders back. Something about her commands authority in this room, but she looks so soft and inviting at the same time. "I see all possibilities," she says. "All the threads of futures, all the things that can come to pass. I see them all."

"Are you God?" I ask my voice barely a whisper.

She laughs and her laugh feels like bubbles from the champagne I sipped at a party once. "Never mind my title, Annie. Listen to what I'm telling you." I nod, indicating I will listen. "Hundreds of thousands of people die every day around the world. I don't have time to see them all or intervene in them all. I watch ones that involve children or violence. In your case," she reaches out and lays a soft hand on my arm. "It involved both."

I resist the urge to tell her I am not a child. Wasn't that the argument I was just making? I am a child. A child whose death leaves a mother without a child. The tears pick up speed and make it a little harder to see the edges of my visitor.

"I know this is hard, Annie, but I saw what could happen here. I watched all the possible futures play out. If you didn't go into that front door, Anthony would've moved into that space. His father eventually comes looking for him. In some of those possible futures, three people die, including you. In some of the futures, four people die, including your mother."

She takes her hand back and uses it to rub her face. She suddenly looks exhausted. "I never liked the idea of letting the recently deceased intervene in their own fate, but this was a risky choice I decided to take. This situation in which your ghost alerts you and agitates Anthony resulted in only one death."

"You knew I was going to die?" Tears flow faster,

blurring my vision. "Are you telling me zero deaths wasn't an option?" I ask, my voice quaking on the tears.

She sighs. "Oh, honey, I wish that it was. But death isn't the only thing I'm considering here. After this scenario, Anthony goes to jail. I know you aren't worried about him right now, but jail is a roof over his head that is away from his abusive father."

"But he gets to go on living," I sputter. My anger is hot and overwhelming in this form. I wipe the tears from my face and shake my head. "He gets to wake up tomorrow."

"So does your mother." That takes the anger away like pouring water on a campfire. I can feel the steam of it leaving my body.

She waves her hand. "I'm not here to get your opinion on the path I chose," she says, her voice hardening. "What's done is done."

"You knew I would fail." I think that's what hurts the most. I tried my hardest to get it right and I was doomed all along.

She shakes her head. "No, that's not true. There was a small chance you would find another path, but even that didn't have an ending I particularly liked." She stands up, brushing her hands down the front of her dress as if checking to make sure it is laying correctly on her thin frame. "This path was the best chance we had at only one death and I was willing to risk it."

Anger floods back into my veins and I stare down at my lap. I let myself feel the hot ball of energy and jump to my feet. "This is a messed-up system," I yell. Just looking at her makes some of the anger dissipate. I can't explain it other than to say it's really hard to stay mad at this woman for some reason. "I'm just supposed to be ok with my death because it gets Tony out of a bad situation? I'm just supposed to be ok with all of this?"

"No, dear. You don't have to be anything anymore. That anger you're feeling is a remnant of your physical being. It's not as strong here as it was on earth and it will not be possible at all once we leave the in-between." She steps closer to me and wraps her arm around my shoulder again, pulling me close. "You don't have to hear anything I said and you don't have to let it change your opinion. I just wanted you to know that there are millions of living beings out there, each like a string. Each of those strings can come together into countless tapestries. One string can never see the entire picture by herself. I wouldn't expect you to understand the masterpiece I'm creating." She pulls back and smiles at me, suddenly looking very much like a teenager. "I just like to explain myself every once in a while."

She takes a step away from me, toward the wall. "Are you coming, dear?" she asks.

"Coming where?"

"To the other side, of course. I told you, this is just the in-between. Useful for processing or for having conversations with me that other beings may not want us to have." She winks. "But not a permanent home." She holds out her hand. "Come with me to the other side. Maybe that will help you let go of the pain your earthly body is telling you to feel."

No pain does sound like a good idea. I take a step forward, reaching my hand out toward her. "Are you talking about heaven?"

"Something like that," she says with another wink.

I nod, slip my hand into hers, and feel absolutely nothing as the entire room fades to black.

About the Author

Tabatha Shipley is an author, avid reader, and book addict from Arizona. She has an amazing husband, two remarkable children, and one really quirky dog. She can often be found on social media raving about whatever book she is most recently obsessed with. Find her to join in on the obsession and add to her TBR with your favorite titles.

tabathashipleybooks.com